"You have too many clothes on," Aidan murmured.

Lily crawled out of her seat and retrieved a pair of blankets from the overhead bin. The cabin was silent and dark, the flight attendants busy in the galley. She sat down next to him and handed him one.

He chuckled softly, drawing her back onto his lap. "Good idea." Aidan pulled the blanket around them and worked at the buttons on her blouse.

Lily stared up into his eyes. Suddenly she felt a bit light-headed. "I think we need more privacy," she whispered. "I'll meet you in the bathroom. Wait for a minute or two and then come back."

She rebuttoned her blouse and crawled off him, then tiptoed down the aisle. She wasn't afraid, and that's what surprised her most. Lily had spent years being fearful of one thing or another. Maybe it was the alcohol, or the altitude—or simply the man himself. But Lily knew exactly what she wanted—no doubts, no insecurities.

A few seconds later Aidan knocked at the door. Lily opened it without hesitation. She was going to have this man, here and now. And she was determined she wouldn't regret it tomorrow.

Blaze™

Dear Reader,

What's my fantasy? I have more than a few. How about a live-in masseuse, or a cat that doesn't shed. A computer that can type the words directly from my brain to my word processing program without me having to lift a finger. I wouldn't mind having a coffee bar in my kitchen with a barista to run it. And I'd love a car that cleaned itself. So none of my fantasies involve sex, but sometimes a girl just needs help with the everyday stuff.

In *Incognito*, I got a chance to explore the naughty side of fantasies. Lily Hart makes one of her fantasies come true when she has the chance to step outside herself and become the kind of woman who'd seduce a man at first sight. And it all happens at 20,000 feet!

I hope you enjoy her story. And I hope you get the chance to make one of your forbidden fantasies come true.

Happy reading,

Kate Hoffmann

KATE HOFFMANN
Incognito

HARLEQUIN®

TORONTO • NEW YORK • LONDON
AMSTERDAM • PARIS • SYDNEY • HAMBURG
STOCKHOLM • ATHENS • TOKYO • MILAN • MADRID
PRAGUE • WARSAW • BUDAPEST • AUCKLAND

ISBN-13: 978-0-373-79410-2
ISBN-10:   0-373-79410-X

INCOGNITO

ABOUT THE AUTHOR

Kate Hoffmann has been writing for Harlequin Books since 1993. Over that time, she's published nearly sixty titles for Harlequin Blaze, Harlequin Temptation, Harlequin anthologies and continuities, and various other lines. When not writing, Kate is involved in musical and theater activities in her community. She lives in southeast Wisconsin with her two cats, Tally and Chloe, and enjoys golf, genealogy and talking on the phone with her sister.

Books by Kate Hoffmann

HARLEQUIN BLAZE
234—SINFULLY SWEET
  "Simply Scrumptious"
279—THE MIGHTY QUINNS: MARCUS
285—THE MIGHTY QUINNS: IAN
291—THE MIGHTY QUINNS: DECLAN
340—DOING IRELAND!
356—FOR LUST OR MONEY
379—YOUR BED OR MINE?

HARLEQUIN SINGLE TITLES (The Quinns)
REUNITED
THE PROMISE
THE LEGACY

HARLEQUIN TEMPTATION
847—THE MIGHTY QUINNS: CONOR
851—THE MIGHTY QUINNS: DYLAN
855—THE MIGHTY QUINNS: BRENDAN
933—THE MIGHTY QUINNS: LIAM
937—THE MIGHTY QUINNS: BRIAN
941—THE MIGHTY QUINNS: SEAN
963—LEGALLY MINE
988—HOT & BOTHERED
1017—WARM & WILLING

To my wonderful, patient, insightful editor, Brenda Chin, who can always find a way to make my words work—even when they don't want to.

Prologue

Last Summer

"YOU HAVE our tickets, don't you?"

Lily Hart sighed softly, her meditation interrupted. She was due to get on a plane in a half hour and if she didn't calm herself, the panic attacks would set in the moment she stepped on board. "Yes, Miranda, I have the tickets. Have I ever forgotten the tickets?"

She reached down into her tote and pulled out the ridiculously expensive Italian leather travel wallet that Miranda had given her last Christmas. As she stared at their boarding passes, tucked neatly into the inside pocket, Lily shook her head. This was her life— designer accessories, first-class tickets to Paris, three weeks in a rented six-bedroom apartment on some fancy rue on the Left Bank. This was her life.

Except it wasn't *her* life. She was living the life of Miranda Sinclair, bestselling novelist. As Miranda's research assistant, social secretary and girl Friday, it was Lily's responsibility to see that Miranda's life was as close to worry-free as possible. And for that, she was paid quite handsomely.

A good-paying job shouldn't come at such a high price, Lily mused. Miranda was Lily's godmother and she'd been her legal guardian since Lily's parents divorced fourteen years ago. Miranda had offered her a home, a place to live when her parents had decided to leave the States. Miranda needed her, more than anyone had ever needed her before, and Lily ought to be grateful.

"I'm sorry," Lily murmured. "I didn't mean to snap. You know how I feel about flying."

Miranda reached out and patted Lily's hand. In addition to providing a home, Miranda had paid Lily's college tuition and she'd given her a job when she got out of school. Lily *was* grateful. Yet she couldn't help but wonder what it might be like to have a life all her own.

"Look," Miranda murmured, nodding in the direction of a man sitting on a sofa on the other side of the first-class lounge. "Gorgeous, no?"

Lily turned to Miranda and frowned. "Stop. I thought we decided you wouldn't do that anymore."

"Just look." She pointed a perfectly manicured finger, then straightened, tucking her ash-blond hair behind her ear. Even though she'd just turned fifty-four, Miranda acted more like a big sister than a parent figure. She certainly didn't look much older than Lily's twenty-seven years. "That is a very fine specimen."

Lily refused the order. For the past few years, Miranda had been intent on finding a man for Lily. Apparently, she hadn't fully approved of the men Lily occasionally found for herself—nice, stable, slightly boring men who wouldn't cheat and wouldn't hurt her. Miranda preferred another type of man—passionate, temperamental, creative—the typical bad boy.

"God, he *is* gorgeous. You know who that is, don't you? That's Aidan Pierce. Hollywood's new *enfant terrible*. Three hit films in as many tries. Every producer in town is sending him projects to direct. How old do you think he is?"

Reluctantly, Lily glanced up and fixed her gaze on the man in question. Her breath suddenly caught in her throat and she was forced to look away—or faint from lack of oxygen.

Living in L.A., she'd seen her share of beautiful men. But she'd always managed to discount them all because they didn't meet the image of perfection she kept in her head. Aidan Pierce came as close to perfect as any man she'd ever set eyes upon.

Swallowing hard, she forced a smile. "Too young for you."

"I'm thinking of changing my rules. I no longer think it would look pathetic for me to date men under the age of thirty." Miranda sat back in her chair and sniffed. "He wouldn't be too young for you. Why don't we go over and introduce ourselves? Offer to buy him a drink."

She moved to stand, but Lily grabbed her arm and pulled her back down. "No, stop it!" She felt a flush creep up her cheeks.

Miranda sighed dramatically. "You know I adore you, darling, but you can't live with me for the rest of your life. You need to get out in the world and enjoy yourself."

"And fixing me up with strange men is going to do that?"

Miranda grudgingly picked up her copy of *Vogue* and flipped through the pages. "I'd hardly call him strange. When was the last time you had sex?"

"None of your business," Lily muttered.

With Miranda's attention distracted, Lily had a chance to observe Aidan Pierce silently. He was dressed casually, in cargo shorts, a faded cotton shirt rolled up at the sleeves and flip-flops. His hair was mussed in a way that made him look as if he'd just rolled out of bed to catch his flight. She could see the shadow of a two- or three-day beard on his chiseled jaw.

A shiver skittered down her spine as she speculated about the body beneath the comfortable clothes. There were women in this world, in L.A., who knew what Aidan Pierce looked like naked—women who had probably touched him in all sorts of tantalizing ways.

A tiny moan slipped from her throat and she covered it with a cough, then glanced over at Miranda. To her dismay, Miranda was watching her, a smug smile on her face. "What?" Lily muttered.

"So you do find him attractive," she said.

"Of course. Who wouldn't?" She looked over at Aidan again, only to see a beautiful young woman plop down on his lap. He squirmed uneasily beneath her, but she refused to budge. "See, he has a girlfriend. He's taken."

Miranda went back to her magazine. "It'll never last. I read in the tabloids that he dates all the most beauti-

ful actresses in Hollywood and then dumps them a
month or two later. His problem is he needs a real
woman. Like you."

"I don't think he'd be interested in me," Lily murmured. Though Miranda had done her best to turn Lily
into a beauty, Lily still felt…ordinary.

Miranda twisted in her chair and leveled her gaze on
Lily. "Have you learned nothing from writing that
book? You can seduce any man you want, you just have
to have confidence in your sex appeal."

Lily shook her head. "I didn't write *The Ten-Minute
Seduction,* you did."

For the past year, Lily had helped Miranda write a
sex manual, a book that instructed women on the most
effective way to seduce a man. Miranda was known for
her bestselling legal thrillers, but for some unknown
reason, she'd felt compelled to switch genres. Knowing
her publishers wouldn't approve, she'd sold the book
using a pseudonym—Lacey St. Claire.

"You know you wrote most of it," Miranda said.
"The book is really yours. And the copyright will be
yours, too. So all the royalties will come to you."
Miranda held up her hand. "I won't hear another word
about it." She put on a pout that was all too familiar to
Lily. "I would have thought you'd have learned something. Anything."

Lily frowned as a slow realization dawned. "What
do you mean?"

Miranda shrugged. "Nothing. Nothing at all."

"Was that all part of your scheming?" Lily demanded. "Did you make me write that book so that I'd know how to seduce a man?"

Miranda pursed her lips. "Well, I didn't expect it to be so good. I just thought I'd put it in a drawer and forget about it. But it *was* good, Lily. Your research combined with my experience made the book publishable. So sue me. I thought I was doing you a favor."

Crossing her arms over her chest, Lily slumped back in her chair. "The meddling stops right now, Miranda. You know how much I love you, but this has got to stop. Do you know how hard I worked on that book? I thought I was helping you and you were just tricking me."

"And when the book comes out next year, you'll be a published author and you'll have a man." Miranda stood and tucked her purse beneath her arm. "I'm going to go get us a few drinks. You're so much easier to manage on a flight after you've tossed back a few cocktails."

Lily watched as her godmother crossed to the bar. She'd dreamed of becoming published, but not this way, not with some sex book. For six months now, she'd been working on her own novel, a simple story about a young girl searching for her place in the world. But between Miranda's schedule and her own insecurities, she hadn't found much time to work.

She watched as Miranda wandered over to Aidan and introduced herself. She nodded in Lily's direction and Aidan gave her a brief look, then turned his attention back to Miranda.

"I have got to get a life of my own," she muttered. She would. As soon as they got back from Paris, she'd look for an apartment. And then, maybe, if a guy like Aidan Pierce glanced in her direction, she'd have the courage to walk up to him and say hello.

1

This summer

"LADIES AND GENTLEMEN, welcome to our premiere service between Los Angeles and New York. While we're preparing for take-off, your flight attendants will be serving beverages. Our scheduled departure of 9:30 p.m. has been pushed back twenty minutes, but the captain assures us that we will be arriving in New York right on time."

The bell dinged and Lily pinched her eyes shut, her white-knuckled hands clutching at the arms of her seat. This was the part she always hated, the waiting, the time between the moment she strapped herself in and the moment the jet lifted off the ground.

Though she'd nearly conquered her aversion to flying about a year ago, her trip to Paris with Miranda had renewed every fear and then doubled it. They'd lost an engine somewhere over the Atlantic and had been forced to make an emergency landing in Ireland. Lily had refused to get back on the plane and had taken a combination of boats and trains to Paris. When it came

time to go home, she'd returned home the same way—
the *QE* II across the Atlantic followed by a cross-
country train trip. Since then, she'd refused to get on a
plane.

She glanced down at the self-help book that lay open
on her tray table. She'd read six books in the past two
months, seen a psychologist and a psychiatrist and
attended two seminars that guaranteed success in con-
quering a fear of flying.

"Airline travel is the safest mode of travel," she murmured to herself, pushing her glasses up the bridge of her
nose. Yeah, right. That would make her feel so much better
when plummeting from twenty thousand feet.

Had Lily been given a choice, she might have taken
the train to New York. But Miranda had insisted that her
fears were unfounded. She just needed to get back on the
horse—which would have been a reasonable alternative
in Lily's mind. L.A. to New York via wagon train. When
was the last time anyone died in a fiery wagon train crash?

In the end, Lily was forced to agree. Her fears were
childish and she needed to conquer them before they
completely paralyzed her. But that didn't mean she'd
be unprepared for disaster. She grabbed the emergency
card from the pocket in front of her and tried to focus
on the information. Why didn't they just give everyone
a parachute? Then if anything bad happened, they
could all jump.

She waved one of the flight attendants over to her
seat. "I think I'm going to need something to drink after
all. If it's not too late."

"We're still waiting for a few first-class passengers to board. What can I get you?"

"Vodka," Lily said. "Two of those little bottles in a glass of ice with just a splash of cranberry juice." Lily forced a smile and sat back in her seat. This was all her fault. She'd made a vow a year ago to move out of Miranda's house and make a life of her own. But the time had never been right.

Miranda had always been in the middle of some crisis or another. Now her godmother was three months late on a deadline and had convinced herself the only place she could possibly finish the book was her summer house in the Hamptons. So Lily had been ordered to go on ahead and open the place.

She reached into her bag and pulled out a small photo album. She'd made the album in a pteromerhanophobia workshop she'd taken last month. The participants had been asked to select photos representing all the things they wanted to do in the future. During a plane trip, they were supposed to find a photo and focus on it.

Lily flipped through the album. There was a picture of the Great Wall of China, her ultimate travel destination. And another of a cute little dog—she'd always wanted a dog, but Miranda was allergic. And there was a photo of a model in a sexy bathing suit. Someday, she'd lose twenty pounds and look just like that.

Lily paused, her gaze falling on the photo of Aidan Pierce she'd cut out of *Premiere*. Someday she'd find a man who made her heart flutter as much as he had.

Since seeing him from across the airport lounge a year ago, Lily had followed his career in the magazines. She'd bought all his movies on DVD and read everything she could find about his social and professional life. And occasionally, she'd allow herself a fantasy or two about what it might be like to have a man like Aidan in her bed.

The flight attendant returned with Lily's drink and set it in front of her, placing the tumbler on top of a napkin. "I'll have to collect that before we take off."

A man passed behind the attendant and she smiled as he bumped against her with his bag. Lily took a sip of her vodka and watched as the passenger searched for an empty overhead bin. He turned and she caught sight of his profile.

She sucked in a sharp breath and the vodka went down wrong, causing a fit of coughing. Gasping for breath, Lily slumped down in her seat and covered her mouth with the napkin.

The flight attendant bent closer. "Are you all right?" she asked.

Lily waved her hand, tears now streaming down her face. Of all the possible people to walk onto her flight, why did it have to be him? She risked a glance up and found Aidan Pierce watching her, an odd look on his face. He glanced at his boarding pass, then looked directly at the numbers above her head.

"No," she said in a silent plea. Not the seat next to her. There were plenty of other places for him to sit. He couldn't possibly be sitting next to her, could he? He showed his boarding pass to the flight attendant and she stepped aside, pointing to the seat next to Lily's.

Lily turned to stare out the window, desperately willing herself to calm down and act like a normal human being. But when she turned back around, she came face-to-face with Aidan's crotch as he reached up to put his bag in the overhead compartment.

His cotton shirt was unbuttoned at the bottom, offering her a view of his belly. Her eyes drifted from the line of hair above his waistband to the bulge in his cargo pants and then back up again. Lily quickly turned away, fixing her attention out the window again.

Suddenly, dying in a mass of twisted steel and burning jet fuel seemed to be an acceptable alternative to flying all the way to New York next to Aidan Pierce. He plopped down beside her. They were so close she could feel the heat of his body, smell the scent of his cologne. She wanted to reach out for her drink, but she was afraid her hand might be trembling too much to pick up the glass.

"It's nice to have you with us again, Mr. Pierce. Can I get you a drink?"

"I'll have a beer," he said.

Oh God. He didn't sound the way he was supposed to sound. She hadn't met him that day at the airport, but she'd watched him interviewed on *E!* and he always seemed so aloof, his voice so careful and measured, kind of self-absorbed. Now, he sounded like a nice guy.

Lily clutched her fingers together in her lap and realized her photo book was still open. She snapped it shut, then dropped it into her tote bag. How long could she possibly sit here without speaking? Sooner or later, someone would have to say something. They couldn't ignore each other for the entire six-hour flight.

"Relax. Nothing is going to happen."

Lily shoved her glasses up the bridge of her nose and gave him a feeble smile. "I-I'm not scared."

He chuckled and then pointed to the book still resting on her tray table. *"The Pteromerhanophobic Traveler,"* he murmured. "Quite a title. Catchy. I'd assume by the little cartoon of the smiling airplane that the book is about people who can't get enough of flying?"

For a moment she relaxed enough to really look at him—his shaggy dark hair and his sculpted mouth, pale blue eyes that seemed to see right through her. In comparison to the buttoned-down business attire most men in first class wore, his lived-in clothes made him look dangerous.

A shiver skittered down her spine. Lily had read thousands of romantic descriptions of male beauty, from Jane Austen to Joan Collins, but for the life of her, she couldn't recall one that did this man justice. He was, for all intents and purposes, perfect.

"I-I'm sorry," she murmured. "You're right. I'm not a very good flyer." But her tension had nothing at all to do with her fear of flying. She'd never been good with extremely handsome men. They always made her feel…clumsy and inept. And handsome men, especially men with beautiful smiles and even more beautiful eyes, made her lose her capacity to think in a rational manner. She always seemed to lose herself in thoughts of what they might look like naked.

"If anything is going to happen," he said, "it'll happen in the first few minutes after takeoff."

"Yes, I know. In the first ninety seconds," Lily said. "So if we're going to die, it's going to happen really soon. That makes me feel better." She glanced over at him to see a smile break across his face.

"Now you're beginning to make me scared."

"I'm sorry," she murmured.

He chuckled. "Why do you keep apologizing?"

"I'm sorry." She took a sharp breath, then forced another smile.

A flight attendant stopped beside Aidan's seat and gave him a warm smile as she set his drink down. Lily glanced across the aisle at another female passenger whose gaze was fixed intently on Aidan. It seemed every woman in his general vicinity found his drink order endlessly fascinating.

She sneaked a better look at his profile. So he shared some qualities with your basic Greek god, but handsome men were a dime a dozen in Los Angeles. She'd just never been so close to one. His elbow grazed hers and Lily gathered her resolve, refusing to move her arm off the armrest of her seat.

He turned back to her and she quickly averted her eyes as he caught her staring. "Would you like another?" he asked.

"Yes," Lily said without thinking.

"Double vodka with a splash of cranberry juice?" the flight attendant asked.

"Just cranberry juice," Lily replied, a blush rising in her cheeks. Already, the vodka had calmed her nerves and warmed her blood. But it wouldn't do to have him thinking she was a lush.

"With just a little vodka," Aidan said.

"I—I really don't drink," Lily said. "Only when I fly."

"Me, too," he replied. "Since we're going to get drunk together, maybe I should introduce myself. My name is Aidan. Aidan Pierce."

"I'm Lily Hart," she said. She carefully placed her fingers into his palm. The moment she touched him, Lily felt a current race through her body. Frowning, she pulled her hand away, clenching her fingers into a fist. "Nice to meet you," she murmured.

If only she knew how to flirt. There were probably ten or fifteen women on this flight who'd give up a year's salary to be sitting exactly where she was. This man was going to be completely wasted on her.

Lily had never needed to flirt. It had never been required for the men who usually found her attractive. But a guy like Aidan probably expected it, maybe even enjoyed it—the witty banter, the offhand caresses, the veiled come-ons. Lily realized if she didn't at least make an attempt, he'd walk away thinking she was…odd.

The flight attendant reappeared with her drink. Aidan handed her the cranberry juice, then he held up his beer in a toast. "To our safe arrival in New York."

Lily gave him a hesitant smile. This wasn't going that badly. In fact, if she wasn't mistaken, *he* was flirting with *her*.

"So why are you headed to the other coast?" Aidan asked.

"I'm taking a little vacation," Lily said. "In the Hamptons."

"I have friends in the Hamptons," he said. "It's pretty wild in the summer. Lots of Hollywood people. So, are you staying with friends or did you rent a place?"

"I—I have a house. I mean, it's my family's house. Well, not really my family, but—I've been going there since I was fourteen. It's near Eastport." She took a sip of her drink. This was a conversation. Now it was time to ask him a question. "And where are you going?"

"The city," he said. "I have a place in SoHo. Actually, I was supposed to have a meeting on this flight, but it was canceled at the last minute. And you must have gotten her seat." He grinned. "Kind of a happy coincidence, don't you think?"

And that was a compliment. Oh God, it was, wasn't it? Or could she simply be reading a deeper meaning into his words? This was exactly how her fantasies always started, except she wasn't usually drunk and she always looked like she'd just stepped out of the pages of a fashion magazine. But this was close enough.

"Feeling better?" he asked.

"A little," Lily said. She reached out to set her drink down, but in her excited state, she missed the edge of the tray table and the glass slipped out of her hand. It tumbled off to the side and landed on Aidan's leg, splashing her drink all over the front of his cargo pants.

Mortified, Lily grabbed a napkin and dabbed at the damp spot then realized where she was dabbing. She looked up into his gaze and caught his bemused smile.

"Sorry," she murmured.

"I can see we're going to have to monitor your consumption." Aidan took the glass from between his legs and set it down. Lily didn't want another drink. Nor did she want to continue to make a fool of herself in front of this man. Suddenly, she felt the need to throw some cold water on her face and regroup.

She bent down and grabbed her tote, then stood. But as she did, her bag caught on the edge of Aidan's tray table and his bottle of beer tumbled over, sending another round of drinks into his lap. "Sorry," she murmured as she crawled over him into the aisle.

When she reached the bathroom, she stumbled inside and locked the door behind her. Lily sat down on the toilet seat and reached into her bag for one of her phobia books. But instead, she pulled out a hot-off-the-press copy of *The Ten-Minute Seduction*.

The book had hit the stores last week to little or no fanfare. She had hoped it might be a success after all the hard work she'd put into it. But really, what woman would need a book like this? Most men didn't need to be seduced. They were usually quite willing to engage in sex whenever and wherever and with whomever.

"*I* need this book," Lily murmured. She opened it up and scanned the first chapter.

Step one, carefully choose a target. Not every man can be seduced. A man who is completely secure and happy in his relationship with the woman in his life may willingly engage in flirtation, but will not be tempted to go further, even if you strip off every last bit of clothing and offer yourself to him on a platter.

She blinked, then looked up at her reflection in the mirror. For all she knew, he could be dating or committed or secretly engaged. Though he seemed to be interested. But then, men in Hollywood cheated all the time. Paging through the book, she found the pertinent section on flirting and read it silently.

Flirtation is a careful balancing act. Show too much interest and you'll scare him off. Show too little and you'll never get past the preliminaries. Make eye contact and then hold it just a few seconds longer than proper before glancing away. Lean in as you speak and if you can, accidentally touch him. A clever combination of confidence and mystery will tempt any man.

Lily moaned. Yes, she'd written these words, but they'd come from careful research, not from real-life experience. She set the book on the edge of the sink and stood up, regarding her reflection in the mirror. The glasses would have to go. She dropped them in her bag, then pulled the elastic from her haphazard ponytail. With trembling fingers, she unbuttoned the next two buttons on her blouse, exposing a bit more skin and just a hint of cleavage.

"Better," she murmured. But it wasn't Lily Hart staring back from the mirror. If only she could become another person entirely, for just the next six hours. Could it be that difficult to play a part? L.A. was all about perception, people pretending to be something they weren't in order to get what they wanted.

Could she push aside her own inhibitions and see if there was a seductress buried somewhere deep inside her? As a single woman living in L.A., she'd have to get herself some kind of "game" if she ever planned on attracting a man like Aidan. Why not take advantage of the situation and see where it led?

Every woman had this fantasy at one point in her life. How many times had she wondered what it might be like to switch places with a beautiful supermodel or a sexy actress, to be the object of every man's secret desires? And she had nothing to lose. She'd never see Aidan Pierce again after this flight.

"Ladies and gentlemen, the captain has turned on the seat-belt sign in preparation for our departure. Please return to your seats and make sure your belongings are stowed securely in the overhead bins or beneath your seat. The flight attendants will be coming around to pick up your drinks."

It was now or never, Lily thought to herself. Just once, she wanted to go out there and grab what she wanted, even if it meant doing something wild and crazy and completely out of character.

Lily quickly flipped through the book, reading the list of hints she'd so carefully researched. "Scent is important." Reaching into her bag, she searched for her perfume. "Highlight your most striking feature." Lily looked in the mirror. She'd always believed that her mouth was sexy. She had full lips, shaped in a perfect Cupid's bow. The kind of lips Hollywood starlets paid good money for. Lily plucked her lipstick out after her perfume. "Be confident, but not arrogant." That would be more difficult. The outside was easy to change, but she'd been living with her doubts and insecurities for a long time.

"Ladies and gentlemen, this is the captain speaking. We're sixth in line for takeoff. We'll be in the air in about five minutes. The weather is clear and our flying time to JFK will be approximately five and a half hours. Just sit back and relax and we'll have you to your destination before you know it."

Five and a half hours to live a fantasy, to live an adventure that might redefine the rest of her life. This time, she wouldn't be left with regrets. This time she'd seek out her fantasies and make them real. And maybe, by doing that, she'd transform herself into a whole new woman.

AIDAN GLANCED at his watch, then turned around to look down the aisle toward the bathroom. Lily had disappeared nearly ten minutes before and he was ready to ask the flight attendant to check on her. She seemed so frightened by the prospect of flying that he was worried she might have gotten sick or even fainted in the bathroom.

When he'd boarded the plane, Aidan had been looking forward to a quiet, uneventful flight. Now that his in-flight meeting had been canceled, he thought he might be able to relax and catch a little sleep. He'd been going nonstop for nearly a year, working on his latest film.

He glanced down at the front of his pants, soaked through with the mixture of their two drinks. The flight attendant had handed him a wad of napkins when she'd collected what was left of the drinks, but Aidan had resigned himself to being uncomfortable for the rest of the flight.

He'd never met a woman quite as skittish as Lily Hart. Though he was used to being hounded for autographs by giggling female fans and had experienced a fair number of racy proposals, he found all that silliness irritating. So why did he suddenly find it so charming in Lily?

Perhaps because there was no artifice there. She wasn't just playing the part to be coy. She really was a bundle of fears and insecurities. No woman intent on charming him would have spilled two drinks on purpose. Or locked herself in a bathroom for ten minutes.

He drew a deep breath and leaned back in his seat, closing his eyes. She was beautiful, though, beneath those schoolteacher glasses and that careless hairstyle. And he couldn't deny he found her attractive. He'd been in L.A. for far too long and the women there had all started to look alike—long blond hair, trainer-toned bodies with spray-on tans. And personalities so bland that he could barely carry on a conversation.

At first, dating beautiful actresses had been a kick. In high school, he'd never been able to get a pretty girl to give him a second look. He'd been skinny and fashion-challenged and he'd worn glasses. College had been a little better. But these days, a membership at a gym, a competent Hollywood stylist and laser eye surgery had corrected all his problems. Now, he could pretty much attract any woman he wanted. The problem was, he didn't want them once he got them.

So what the hell was he searching for? "Someone real," Aidan murmured. "Something real."

He'd become disenchanted with his life in general, his work, women, even the car he drove. He'd been making hit films, but they weren't important films—they didn't mean anything, they wouldn't last. His relationships had fallen into the same pattern, flashy on the surface and devoid of any true emotion. And hell, he drove a gas-guzzling SUV just because it looked cool. What was that all about?

Maybe that was why he found Lily Hart so intriguing. She was real, with all her quirks and mannerisms. She'd made a complete fool out of herself and yet he found that utterly charming.

And she was pretty, too. She wore barely any makeup; her pale ivory skin was almost flawless. Her dark hair, pulled away from her face, made her features even more striking. But it was mouth that he found most alluring. It was perfectly shaped, untouched by all those silly injections.

Aidan scolded himself inwardly. Why did he automatically focus on her looks? Was this what L.A. had done to him, turned him into a shallow, superficial jerk? The woman sitting next to him wasn't just a bunch of features thrown together for his viewing enjoyment. Hollywood was insidious, like a drug that lured you in only to make your life worthless.

That's why he had felt compelled to return to New York. A dose of life in the real world always seemed to clear his mind and focus his thoughts. Aidan needed to remember the days when he had to pull pennies out of the sofa just to buy a cup of coffee.

The plane began to move slowly down the taxiway and Aidan pushed out of his seat and walked back to the bathroom. He rapped softly on the door. "Lily? Are you all right in there?"

An instant later, the door swung open and he found himself staring into the most striking green eyes he'd ever seen. He took a step back, certain that he'd knocked at the wrong door. But then he realized he was looking at Lily. She'd removed her glasses and let her hair down, the wavy dark strands curling around her neck. Her face, once pale and tense, was now flushed with color and her lips were painted a seductive shade of red.

He nervously cleared his throat. "You're supposed to be in your seat. We're going to be taking off soon."

She smiled at him, regarding him from beneath long dark lashes. "Thanks," she murmured.

He stepped aside and let her pass, then followed her down the aisle. His gaze dropped to her backside, the fabric of her skirt clinging to her curves like a second skin. Lily flipped up her tray table and buckled her seat belt.

"Feel better?" Aidan asked.

"Yes," she said calmly. "Much."

"What were you doing in there?"

"Ah—meditating," Lily replied. "It's great for relieving stress."

Aidan couldn't believe the change in her. She seemed to have conquered her nerves and he suspected she might have gulped down a Xanax or two while she was in the bathroom. But as the plane turned onto the end of the runway and the wing flaps whirred, he saw her stiffen, proof that her calm demeanor was only skin-deep.

Aidan reached out and took her hand, lacing her fingers through his. "Look at me," he said. She turned and met his gaze. "Just keep your eyes on mine and listen to my voice. There's nothing to be afraid of. I've taken this flight a hundred times and I'm still here."

"You—you have beautiful eyes," she murmured. "And long lashes."

"I was just thinking that about you," Aidan replied. "And your mouth. It's…"

"What?" Lily asked.

"Very…kissable."

"Really?"

"Yes," Aidan said, his gaze dropping to her lips. "Really." He felt the plane begin to accelerate down the runway and he reached out and took her face between his hands. Leaning forward, Aidan kissed her gently, his tongue tracing along the crease of her lips until she sighed and opened beneath his assault.

As the plane gained speed, the kiss became more intense, Aidan exploring the sweet recesses of her mouth, drinking in the taste of her. He drew her closer, but her seat belt got in the way. He was almost frantic for more, the sensation of the plane lifting from the ground adding to the rush of adrenaline that surged through his veins.

The engines roared, obliterating the sound of his pulse pounding in his head. A tiny moan slipped from her throat, but the kiss continued. Aidan knew they were probably making a scene, but he was past caring. Instinct had taken over and he couldn't seem to stop himself.

A ping sounded over the PA system and the bell startled them both out of their sudden lapse into passion. She slowly pulled back, her mouth damp, her lips twitching. "What was that?" she asked.

"If you have to ask, then I guess I didn't do it right," he said.

"No, I—I meant that bell."

Aidan pointed to the light panel above their heads. "The seat-belt sign," he said. "You are now free to get up and move about the cabin."

"I'll be right back," Lily said, grabbing her bag again and unbuckling her seat belt.

He stood up and stepped into the aisle, then decided to take the window seat after she'd left. A few moments later, the flight attendant stopped by, returning the drinks that she'd collected before takeoff. She also set a plate of cheese and fruit on Lily's tray table. "I'll be back to get your dinner order in a few minutes," she said.

He grabbed a grape and popped it in his mouth, chewing slowly as he considered all that had happened since he'd stepped on the plane. Aidan had never been one to indulge in anonymous sexual encounters, but then, he'd never met a woman like Lily Hart. His first intent in kissing her was merely to distract her. But the moment her lips parted beneath his, Aidan's intentions had changed.

He couldn't deny the attraction and he couldn't help but be a bit curious as to what would happen if he acted on it. This was dangerous territory, the kind of scenario that most men found arousing, yet never experienced in real life.

Lately, Aidan had tried to be more cautious with his sex life, more discerning. He'd grown tired of having his social life splashed across the pages of every Hollywood magazine. Though his publicist loved it, Aidan was frustrated that his personal life had become better entertainment than his films.

If he were smart, he'd get up and move to another seat. If he indulged in this little scenario, it was sure to be all over the press in a few days and though most of his other girlfriends enjoyed the coverage, he wasn't sure Lily Hart would feel the same.

When he'd first kissed her, he hadn't expected her to return the kiss with such enthusiasm. Nor had he predicted his own reaction. Aidan cursed softly. This was crazy! He'd made a decision to find something real in his life and here he was considering a superficial sexual encounter on an airplane. The Mile-High Club was such a cliché!

He opened his eyes, then pushed out of his seat. When he got back to the bathroom, he knocked softly on the door. This time, when Lily opened it, he recognized her. Aidan glanced both ways, then pushed inside, closing the door behind him.

The bathroom was tiny with barely enough room for the two of them to stand. His body pressed against hers and he was forced to grasp her waist to maintain his balance. "About what happened," he murmured. "I—I was just trying to distract you. I didn't mean to—" He swallowed hard. "I didn't mean to enjoy it…so much." He paused. "Did you enjoy it?"

"Yes," she said, watching him through wide eyes. Her gaze dropped to his mouth, then flitted back up to his eyes again.

Aidan knew what he had to do, what she wanted him to do, and what he found impossible to resist. Without a second thought, he brought his mouth down on hers. This time, it wasn't to distract her. This time, his thoughts were completely focused on the sensations of her sweet mouth beneath his.

He'd kissed a lot of women, but it had never been quite like this. There was something forbidden about what they were doing, something dangerous, that made the simple act of kissing seem so much more intense.

He felt her fingers tangle in his hair and a groan slipped from his throat as he pulled her against him.

Maybe that was it. Had they been standing at her front door, this would be just an ordinary kiss. But the anticipation of what might happen between them next was making this all more thrilling than it really was. It made sense, but at the same time, Aidan didn't want to believe it. Maybe he'd simply found a woman he could trust—at least for the next six hours.

He drew back and smoothed her hair away from her face. "We should go back to our seats," he said. "Someone is going to want this bathroom."

She didn't speak, just nodded. Lily grabbed her purse from the sink, then slipped out the door. When he returned to his seat, her eyes were fixed on a book in her lap. He watched as she turned a page, noting the tremor in her hand. Reaching out, Aidan drew a finger across the soft skin below her wrist and she turned to look at him.

"Later," he promised.

2

THE LIGHTS in the first-class cabin were dimmed a few minutes after the dinner service ended. Most of the passengers took the opportunity to catch some sleep. With the time change, they'd arrive in New York just after six in the morning, the beginning of a brand-new day.

But right now, Lily wanted the night to last forever. She and Aidan had shared a bottle of champagne during dinner and to her surprise, she was feeling remarkably relaxed. She suspected the company had something to do with that, as well.

Their dinner conversation had been light and teasing, Lily carefully weaving her web of mystery around her handsome companion. He'd kissed her. Obviously, he found her attractive and that thought gave her the confidence she needed to continue with her "experiment."

If she expected to have a social life, she was going to have to learn to operate like the other women in L.A. She needed to be able to use her seductive powers to get what she wanted. After all, competition for men like Aidan Pierce would be relentless. Lily knew she'd probably never be able to compete for a guy like him in the real world, but right now, he was sitting next to her—and touching her—and kissing *her.*

Though he was curious about her life, he wasn't bothered by her evasive answers. Telling him the truth about who she was and what she did would prove just one thing—her life was incredibly dull.

But Aidan wasn't reluctant to speak about his life. He amused her with little stories of his travel adventures. He'd been all over the world, staying in exotic locales she'd only read about. When he talked about Tahiti, she commented on the beaches and didn't correct him when he assumed she'd been there. When he asked, Lily simply said she'd visited many interesting and exotic places in the world.

"You haven't told me what you do for a living," Aidan said.

Lily took a sip of champagne, attempting a coy smile. "I write," she said. It was the truth. A simplified version of it, at least. "What about you?"

He seemed surprised by the question. Of course, she knew exactly what he did for a living. But she could pretend she didn't. Wouldn't that add a little more mystery to the attraction between them?

"Forget that question," she said. "Let's not talk about work." Lily studied him for a long moment. There was another question that needed to be answered. "Are you married?" Lily knew he wasn't, but he could be involved in a relationship that hadn't been reported in the magazines.

"No," Aidan said. "And you?"

"No," she admitted. "But let's not talk about relationships, either."

"So we can't talk about work or relationships. What's left?"

Lily smiled. "I don't know. Tell me about your childhood."

He picked up her right hand and carefully studied her fingers. Then he drew her hand to his mouth and kissed each fingertip. No man had ever done that to her before and Lily found it strangely provocative. "I had a normal childhood," he said. "Nothing dysfunctional, nothing traumatic. What about you?"

Lily hesitated. She never talked about her childhood, not even to Miranda. She'd managed to bury all the emotions so deeply that they barely even touched her heart anymore. "Mine was perfectly idyllic," she lied. "Next topic. How about favorite color?"

"Blue. Favorite dessert?"

"Lemon meringue pie," Lily replied. "Favorite vacation spot?"

"Your mouth," he murmured.

Lily's breath froze and her mind raced for a witty comeback. Men just didn't talk to her like this! She glanced away, hoping for inspiration, but Aidan hooked his finger beneath her chin and forced her gaze to meet his.

"And yours?" he asked.

"The first-class bathroom on the flight between LAX and JFK," she said, trying to keep her voice from cracking.

This was it. There was no going back. Lily was now an exciting and interesting and adventurous woman, the kind of woman who could seduce a man like Aidan, the kind of woman he'd want.

"So do you plan to return to that spot anytime soon?" he asked. He reached between them and pushed the armrests out of the way, then grabbed her waist and pulled her across his lap.

Lily looked around to see if anyone had noticed, but Aidan cupped her face in his hands and turned her gaze to his. "Don't worry. They're all asleep."

"You've done this before?"

"Never," he said. "But I can't say it hasn't crossed my mind a few times during a particularly boring flight. I usually get seated next to businessmen or grandmothers." He wrapped his arm around her hip and his other hand tangled in her hair.

This time when he kissed her, it was easy and perfect, as if he'd memorized the contours of her mouth and knew just how they fitted together. Lily relaxed in his embrace, enjoying the way he made love to her lips and her tongue. She'd always thought kissing was overrated, two mouths pressed together. But Lily now realized she'd never really been kissed, at least not by a man who took his desires seriously.

With every taste, she could feel his need growing more desperate. She shifted, her backside pressed into his lap and he moaned softly. Emboldened by his reaction, Lily sat up, bracing her hand on his thigh. Parting the front of his shirt, she leaned closer and kissed his chest.

She'd never been so blatantly forward with a man and it felt good. But she wasn't in the real world anymore, she'd been caught inside this fantasy. She didn't have to think before she acted. There were no rules and nothing was out of bounds.

Lily reached for the buttons of her blouse, but he brushed her fingers away, tugging at the fabric until he'd exposed the curve of her shoulder. Aidan bit at the spot beneath her ear, his breath warm against her skin, then trailed his lips to a spot between her breasts. "You have too many clothes on," he murmured.

Lily crawled out of her seat and retrieved a pair of blankets from the overhead bin. The cabin was silent and dark, the flight attendants busy in the galley. She sat down next to him and handed him the blanket.

He chuckled softly, drawing her back onto his lap.

"Now I'm beginning to wonder if *you've* done this before." Aidan pulled the blanket around them both and worked at the buttons of her blouse.

Lily stared up into his eyes. Suddenly, she felt lightheaded, but she drew a deep breath and stopped him from going further. "I think we might need a bit more privacy," she murmured. "I'll meet you in the bathroom. Wait for a minute or two and then come back."

She rebuttoned her blouse and crawled off him, then tiptoed down the aisle. A flight attendant saw her from the galley and stepped out. "Is there anything I can get for you?" she asked.

Lily shook her head. "I'm fine," she replied.

The flight attendant nodded, returning to her coworkers. Lily locked herself in the bathroom, then braced her arms on the edge of the sink. This was it. If she had any inhibitions left, she needed to rid herself of them pretty quickly. A shiver shook her body and she drew a deep breath and looked at herself in the mirror.

She wasn't afraid, and that's what surprised her the most. Lily had spent most of her life being fearful of one thing or another. Maybe it was the alcohol, or the altitude, or the unfamiliar surroundings, but she knew exactly what she wanted—no doubts, no insecurities.

Or maybe it was the man. Aidan had been charming and attentive, treating her like the most captivating woman he'd ever met. It was easy to seduce a man who wanted to be seduced. Lily drew a ragged breath. She'd followed the advice in the book and she now had a willing partner. But was she prepared to go the rest of the way?

A few seconds later, Aidan knocked on the door. Without a second thought, Lily opened it. She wanted this man, here and now. There was no reason to deny her needs—or her fantasies.

THE DOOR clicked shut behind him. The sound was like a starter's pistol, both of them coming together in a flurry of hands and mouths. Lily's fingers clutched at the hem of his shirt and he tugged it over his head. A moment later, the buttons on her blouse were dispatched and Aidan pulled it down over her arms.

He yanked Lily against him, finding her mouth again and furrowing his fingers through her hair. Skin met skin beneath the harsh light from above the sink. He drew back to look into her eyes and at that moment, Aidan was certain Lily was the most beautiful woman he'd ever met.

How could this be happening? When he'd stepped onto the plane a few hours before, he'd expected the usual trip spent sleeping or reading or distractedly watching a movie. But now he was locked in a tiny bathroom, undressing a stranger.

Her lips were damp from his kiss and her hair tumbled around her face. Her breath came in quick gasps. Pressing his forehead to hers, he gently smoothed his hand over her shoulder, then down her chest. When he reached her breast, he cupped it in his palm.

Everything about her was natural, including her perfect breasts. It had been so long since he'd touched a completely real woman and the prospect of making love to her was overwhelmingly exciting.

But it wasn't just her appearance, Aidan mused. Every reaction was honest and unstudied. With other women, he felt as if their responses were designed solely to increase his pleasure, the moans, the sighs, the frantic whispers, scripted like lines in some porno flick. When he touched Lily, she trembled. When he softly bit her neck, her breath caught in her throat. And when she felt pleasure, she sighed.

Aidan slipped his fingers beneath her bra and drew his thumb over her nipple. It was already puckered into a hard peak. Grabbing her waist, he turned her around, then sat down and pulled her between his legs. Her belly was soft, her skin like silk, and he reached up and drew her bra straps over her shoulders.

Lily held her arms over her breasts but he gently captured her hands in his. "You're beautiful," he murmured. "Let me touch you."

Another tiny moan slipped from her throat as he brushed his lips across her nipple through the fabric of her bra. Everything around them seemed to dissolve into a soft haze. He was aware of the sounds of the plane, the whir of a fan above his head, the buzz of the fluorescent lights, the muffled roar of the engines. But his attention was completely focused on her body—and her pleasure.

He smoothed his hands along her thighs, shoving her skirt up to her hips. Pressing his face into the warmth of her body, Aidan kissed her belly and inhaled the sweet scent.

Lily's hands skimmed over his chest, her fingers trembling. She seemed to be transfixed by the feel of his body beneath her touch. Her cheeks were flushed and her breath came in tiny gasps. Though he was certain she'd been with a man before, it seemed as if this was all new to her.

"Have you ever done *this* before?" he asked, suddenly needing to know.

She shook her head, her thick hair a curtain around her face. "No."

Though he'd learned to doubt what usually came out of a woman's mouth, Aidan sensed he could trust Lily. He covered her fingers with his and pressed her hand to his heart. "Me, neither."

A tiny smile curled the corners of her mouth, as if she were pleased by the admission. He stood and pulled her into his embrace, his lips finding hers again. They stumbled as they searched for a comfortable space, their feet tangling together. Frustrated, Aidan circled her waist with his hands and lifted her up to balance her on the edge of the tiny sink.

Grabbing her legs, he wrapped them around his waist and lost himself in the taste of her mouth. Lily braced her hands above her head, her blouse still caught around her wrists, exposing her body to his touch.

Aidan knew they wouldn't be able to stay in the bathroom forever. Yet he didn't want to rush. He'd come prepared, retrieving a condom from his overnight bag before following her into the bathroom.

He slowed his pace, kissing her deeply. His hand slipped beneath the waistband of her skirt and she arched against him. They were still dressed, but it was clear where they were headed.

Instinctively, he began to move against her, his erection rubbing at the spot between her legs. He was glad for the barrier between them. Without it, he would have been far too close to his release. Lily braced her arms behind her and tipped her head back.

"Tell me what you want," he said. He drew her leg up along his hip, the contact between them suddenly more intimate. "This?"

"Oh, yes." Lily sighed, shuddering as she spoke.

At first, she seemed to be so focused on what he was doing to her that she barely moved. But then, she reached around and grabbed his ass, pulling him even closer. The fabric from his pants created a delicious friction against his shaft. Aidan considered himself quite skilled in the bedroom, able to pleasure a woman in a hundred different ways before giving in to his own needs. But when Lily touched him, he felt as though he was experiencing a woman for the first time.

Was it the excitement of doing something so forbidden? Had he become so jaded about sex that it took something a little kinky to turn him on? Or was there something about Lily that made her different from the others? He barely knew her, yet he felt as if they'd been thrown together for a reason.

Her hand slipped beneath his waistband and Aidan groaned. He was so close already, yet he kept tight control over his desire. He wanted to lose himself inside her, but at that moment, Aidan realized it didn't make a difference how or where he found release.

This wouldn't be the last time they shared an experience like this. He didn't have any intention of letting her just walk out of the airport and out of his life forever. He would seduce her again, and not in a cramped airplane bathroom, but in a big soft bed.

She buried her face in the curve of his neck, biting softly as they continued to move against each other. And then, to his surprise, she cried out, her body quivering in his arms, the sound of her orgasm muffled against his skin.

Aidan was stunned. And so, it seemed, was Lily. He stared down into her face and her eyes were wide with wonder. He kissed her gently and she melted against him, her breath still coming in soft gasps.

"How long do you think we can stay in here before someone knocks on the door?" he whispered.

"I don't think we should go just yet," she said. "We're not…done, are we?"

He glanced at his watch. "We still have two more hours until we land. There's a lot we can do with two hours."

"Like what?" Lily teased.

"Anything you want. I'm at your command."

A tiny smile twitched at her lips. "Oh, a slave boy. That's one of my fantasies right there. Kiss me, slave boy."

Aidan growled, then softly bit her lower lip. "I prefer slave assistant."

She laughed, then pressed her mouth to his in a delicious kiss. But her delight was short-lived. A sudden jolt put him off balance and Aidan reached out to steady himself, bracing his arm against the door.

When he looked back at Lily, her eyes were wide with terror. "What was that?"

"I think the earth just moved," he joked. But his joke didn't make her smile. "It's all right. Just a little turbulence."

The plane dropped again, only this time, the jolt was enough to throw him forward. He banged his head on a sharp corner above the sink and a curse slipped from his lips. "Shit. That hurt."

"Are you all right?" Lily asked.

Aidan looked over her shoulder into the mirror. "I think I'm bleeding."

Lily grabbed his chin and examined the scrape on his forehead. Then she leaned over and pulled a paper towel from the dispenser. But when she tried to twist around to turn on the sink, she couldn't move. "Here," she said. "You sit and I'll stand."

He did as he was told, but a third bump sent her sprawling into his arms. "This may be every man's fantasy, but the logistics of it are really tricky," he said, his erection pressed against the soft flesh of her belly.

"Ladies and gentleman, this is the captain speaking. We've run into a patch of rough weather here and we're going to ask that you stay in your seats with your seat belts fastened. We're going to try a different altitude and see if we can get you a smoother ride."

"Rough weather? What does that mean?" Lily asked.

"It means we'd better get dressed and get back to our seats before they come looking for us," he muttered. He should have been disappointed it was going to end so quickly. But Aidan was willing to wait.

As soon as this damn plane touched down, he'd find a quiet, private place where he could enjoy Lily's body for as long as he wanted. Until then, he'd have to convince her that this flight was only the beginning and not the end.

LILY FUMBLED with her seat belt, the clip refusing to fasten properly. Her heart pounded in her chest and she couldn't seem to catch her breath. The bumps were so bad that she was bouncing in her seat. For a moment, she thought she might pass out, but then Aidan sat down beside her.

They'd managed to get their clothes back on, though it was a struggle with the turbulence and the close quarters. Lily had sneaked out of the bathroom first and he'd followed her a minute later.

Seeing her dilemma, he quickly fastened her seat belt then took care of his own. "Don't worry," he said, wrapping his arm around her shoulders. "We'll be fine."

"The plane feels like it's falling," Lily said. She peered out the window. "It's raining. And there's lightning. What if we get hit by lightning? I heard about a plane that got hit by lightning."

"What happened?"

"I don't remember. Maybe I've blocked it out. It must have been bad." Her stomach churned and she felt as if she might throw up. Lily searched through the pocket of the seat in front of her for the airsick bag. When she found it, she clutched it to her chest. "I should have taken the train."

"But then you wouldn't have met me."

"I hate this, I hate this, I hate this," she said. "Last year, I was flying to Paris and we lost an engine."

"A plane can fly with just one engine."

"You don't understand. It fell off the plane, into the ocean." Lily stopped short. She'd been so careful not to reveal too much. But the fear of dying made her babble.

She tried to calm herself, to think of other things— like what had just happened in the bathroom. Her skin prickled with goose bumps as she recalled the feel of him, hot and hard against her body, the thoughts making her even more light-headed.

And then her reaction. She'd experienced release with men before, but never with so little prompting. If it hadn't been for the turbulence, they might have continued with the seduction and she would have enjoyed those pleasures again.

"You were on that flight? I heard about that. Man, that must have been scary." Aidan pressed a kiss to her temple. "What are the odds of that happening again? Microscopically small, I'd say. In fact, you should be happy that happened. Now it's over with. There's no way it can happen to you again."

She glanced over at him. He really was a nice guy. It would have been much simpler to seduce a man who wasn't so sweet, some guy with a macho attitude and an overinflated opinion of himself. At least he'd be easier to leave behind. But Aidan—he'd be hard to forget.

"Maybe that book of yours would help," he suggested. "Would you like me to read to you?"

"Sure," she murmured. She pointed to her bag tucked beneath his seat. The sound of his voice had already calmed her down. And if she could focus on that, then she wouldn't be nearly as scared.

"You must think I'm such a baby," Lily said.

"We all have our fears."

"What are you afraid of?"

He grinned. "I'm not going to tell you. I've worked too hard to make you think I was a stud."

"Tell me," Lily insisted.

"Snakes," he admitted. "And bats. And I'm not real

fond of spiders or centipedes, either. In fact, anything that can kill you with its bite is something I try to avoid."

"A brown bat can catch and eat over six hundred mosquitoes in an hour," she said. The moment the words left her mouth, she knew she'd made a mistake. "I—I did a report on bats when I was a kid. Funny how you remember things like that when you're about to die." Lily groaned inwardly. Maybe she ought to just give up. Playing the part of a seductress wasn't that easy. Still, some men found intelligence a turn-on, didn't they?

Aidan reached down and opened her bag, then pulled out her stack of flying books. *"Conquer Your Fear of Flying,"* he read.

"That one didn't work," Lily said.

"Here's the one with the big title."

"Pteromerhanophobia," Lily said. "That's the fear of flying."

"And what's the fear of really big words?" he muttered.

"Logophobia," Lily said. "Actually, that's just the fear of words in general. Not necessarily big words. Arithmophobia is the fear of numbers. Graphophobia is the fear of writing." He stared at her for a long moment. Too much knowledge was never a good thing. "Sometimes these facts just fly out of my mouth," she said with a laugh. "I don't know why I remember them, but I do."

"How about this one? *Have Fun Flying? Flying with No Fear?*" He picked up another book. "How about—" Aidan went silent and Lily turned to look at him. He was holding the copy of—

"The Ten-Minute Seduction," he read. "This looks interesting." He flipped through the pages.

"It—it's not what you think," Lily said. Frowning, she reached out and took the book from him. "What do you think?"

"That this wasn't all just a spontaneous experience? That you got on this plane determined to seduce someone and I just happened to be close at hand?"

Lily searched for a way to make him understand. He wasn't some lab rat in her bizarre sexual experiment. "It—it's *my* book," she said.

"I know that. It was in your bag."

"I mean, I wrote it. It's mine. I'm…"

"You're Lacey St. Claire?"

"Yes?" She opened the book and pointed to the notes she'd made in the margins. "See. I was just making some notes, in case it goes to a second printing."

He shook his head in disbelief. "I was seduced by the woman who wrote the book on seduction?"

"Yes?" she replied. "Actually, I think you seduced me."

"No, I'm sure it was the other way around." He paused. "And you do this often?"

"No!" Lily said, unable to let that pass. She might be pretending to be a seductress, but she wasn't a slut. "No! Never. I mean, I've been with men, but I don't make it a habit to seduce strangers."

"So, I was the exception, rather than the rule?"

"Yes," Lily said, thankful that he was finally beginning to see the truth. "Most of what I've written comes from scientific studies, not from experience. It's all basic physiology, the attraction between men and women."

"Scientists do studies on seduction? Hell, I definitely would have chosen that for a major in college had I known."

"The study of human sexuality is a very important field. Behavior can be instinctual and reactions predicted."

He took the book from her hands and examined it closely. "So what's your real name? Lacey or Lily?"

"Lily. Lacey is my pen name. To protect my privacy."

"Yeah, I can see why. Ten minutes. Most guys only need two or three before they're ready to go."

"You're angry?"

He shook his head, frowning as he read the back cover copy. "*Confused* would be a better word," he said. "Maybe a little…disconcerted."

Lily took his hand. "Don't be. I don't have any regrets. Do you?"

"You're the expert on seduction. You'll have to tell me how I measured up."

"No!" Lily said. "It's just a book. Authors write about vampires and witches and monsters, but they've never seen them. You're the first man I've actually…seduced."

He took a moment to consider her confession, then nodded. "I guess most men would appreciate a woman who has some book smarts when it comes to sex."

Lily nodded. "Men have techniques for seducing women, right? And they're written down in all those men's magazines and how-to books. Why shouldn't women have the same advantage? It's only fair." She gently pulled the book from his hand and tossed it back into her bag.

"You're right."

By the time they finished their discussion, Lily realized that the turbulence had stopped and the plane was now flying smoothly again. She took his hand and wove her fingers through his. It seemed quite natural to maintain the contact, but she had to wonder why she felt it necessary. In a few more hours, they'd be saying goodbye to each other. And then she'd never see him again.

"Ladies and gentlemen, this is your captain speaking. I'm afraid I have another bit of bad news. We've got fog rolling in over JFK. The airport has just been closed to incoming flights. Because of our fuel situation, we're going to be diverted inland to Hartford, Connecticut. Once the fog clears, we'll get you back on your way."

Lily heard a communal groan go up from the passengers in tourist class. She looked over at Aidan and he shrugged. "The only time fog is dangerous is when you try to land in it, so we're safe." He glanced around the cabin. "I think I need a drink. Do you want one?"

She watched him as he spoke to the flight attendant. For some reason, he found it necessary to be overly charming, as if he were trying to punish Lily for the secrets she'd kept.

Maybe this was for the best, she mused. She'd had her fun and that was the end of it. There would be no thought of making another trip to the bathroom or of carrying on after the plane landed.

Lily fought the urge to grab the book again. Though she knew it by heart, she couldn't recall a chapter on how to deal with the aftereffects of an anonymous seduction. Could she separate her memories of the act itself from thoughts of Aidan? She brushed aside a tiny twinge of regret.

It wouldn't do to second-guess her decision. What was done was done. And she'd gotten exactly what she wanted from him—a fantasy fulfilled.

But suddenly, that wasn't enough to satisfy her. Now, she wanted more.

THE SUN was already up by the time they landed in Hartford. The airline had decided to let the passengers disembark while they waited for a new flight crew to arrive in Hartford. Once the weather cleared, they'd take off again for New York. Aidan grabbed his bag from the overhead bin, then stepped aside to let Lily pass.

It was early morning and he was drunk. He'd spent the last hour of the flight drinking Jack Daniel's and water while he tried to figure out just what the hell Lily Hart was up to. She didn't seem like one of those mercenary women he was always trying to avoid, women who set their sights on a man then did anything and everything required to possess him. What had happened between them seemed perfectly natural, just two people discovering an overwhelming attraction and acting upon it.

But maybe that's what it was—acting. Someone so schooled in the art of seduction could make a man believe anything she wanted, right? Was any of it real? Her fear of flying, the way her hands trembled as she touched him, the claim that she'd never made love on an airplane. Maybe he'd been played.

His gaze fixed on her face, on the pretty features he'd come to appreciate over the past six hours. She was like no other woman he'd ever met, an odd mix of crazy bravado and overwhelming vulnerability. Instinct told him she hadn't planned to seduce him when she got on the plane, but experience warned him not to trust her. Hell, he'd decided to take a break from women, to leave all the superficial attractions behind him, where they belonged—in L.A.

If he only had a little more time, he might be able to figure her out. For some reason, the truth mattered. "Let me get that for you," he said, grabbing her overnight bag. "Do you have much luggage?"

Lily shook her head. "Just that bag."

"You travel light for a woman," he said.

"I have clothes at the house."

They walked through the jetway side by side and silently. But there was a tension crackling between them that couldn't be ignored, the air filled with unexpressed desire. Spending the next few hours together wasn't going to be easy. On the plane, they were in their own little world. Now, they'd landed right back to reality.

Aidan brushed aside the urge to drop their bags and pull her into his arms, losing himself in another kiss.

"Would you like to get some breakfast?" he asked. "We've got some time. And I could really use some coffee."

Lily smiled, then giggled softly. "Me, too. I'm still a little dizzy from the champagne and the lack of sleep."

"I've got to tell you, that's the most fun I've ever had on a cross-country flight."

They were headed for the first-class lounge, assured by the airlines that they'd be back on their way within a few hours. Aidan thought about renting a car and offering Lily a ride to the Hamptons, but he didn't want to risk her refusal.

But as they walked through the gate and into the airport, he realized his time with Lily might be at an end. A woman in an airline uniform stood at the door, holding a card with Lily's name written on it. Lily hadn't seen it and was about to walk right by, when Aidan tapped her on the shoulder. "I think that person is looking for you."

"Are you Miss Lily Hart?" the woman asked.

"Yes."

"I have a message. You're to meet your driver outside the security checkpoint."

"My driver?"

"Yes, ma'am. Have you checked any bags?"

Lily shook her head. "No."

"Then, I hope you enjoyed your flight and that you'll fly with us again soon," she said, nodding.

"Thank you," Lily replied. She stood mutely as she watched the woman walk away. Then she turned to

Aidan and smiled. "So, I guess I'll have to take a rain check on breakfast," she murmured. Lily reached out and took her bag from his hand, then hoisted it over her shoulder. She held out her hand. "It was nice…meeting you, Aidan."

He couldn't help but smile. Meeting? She might as well have been honest and said it was nice seducing him. "Hey, I'll walk you down there," he offered. "I've got some time."

"No, that's not necessary. You don't have to."

Aidan hooked his fingers through the strap of her bag and pulled it off her shoulder. "I could use the exercise." He started off toward the concourse, giving her no choice but to follow him. When she caught up, he reached out and took her hand, lacing his fingers through hers.

"So, what are you going to do in the Hamptons?" he asked. "I mean, besides work?"

"I'm going to relax. Maybe catch up on my reading."

"So you're not planning to go out and seduce another man?"

"No!" Lily cried.

"Well, if you're bored or want something to do, you can always give me a call. You can come into the city and we'll have dinner. Or I'll come out to the Hamptons and we'll have lunch."

When they reached the end of the concourse, the chauffeur was waiting, holding up a card with Lily's name scribbled on it. She stood in front of Aidan, staring at her feet. "So, I guess *this* is it," she said.

"I guess so," he replied. Goodbyes after a one-night stand were always a bit uncomfortable, though this didn't really qualify as a full night. Maybe this was just a half-night stand since they hadn't managed to go all the way with her seduction.

Usually, Aidan was anxious to escape after spending the night with a woman. Now, he wasn't. He wanted to spend the next two or three hours saying goodbye to Lily—and making sure he'd see her again. But she seemed perfectly content just to walk away.

She pushed up on her toes and gave him a quick kiss on the cheek. "Take care, Aidan."

"You, too, Lily."

He watched as she walked toward the driver, then remembered he hadn't given her his cell-phone number. "Lily! Wait up."

She stopped and turned. When he reached her, he held out his hand. "I forgot to give you my number. Do you have a cell phone?"

Lily dropped her bag on the floor, then searched through her tote. When she found it, she handed it to him. Aidan put his number into her memory dial, then snapped the phone shut. "There. Call me. Sometime. Anytime. Soon."

She nodded as she tucked the phone back into her tote. "Or you could call me," she suggested.

"I don't have your number." He reached in his back pocket for his cell and handed it to her, but she shook her head. "I can't program those things." She recited her number and Aidan put it into the phone's memory.

Then she glanced over her shoulder. "I really should go. He's waiting."

"Right," Aidan said. He shoved his phone back inside his pocket, then leaned forward and grabbed her arms. Pulling her body against his, Aidan furrowed his fingers through Lily's hair. A heartbeat later, his mouth met hers. The kiss was swift, but intense, Aidan making sure that it was something she'd remember—and long to repeat.

When he was finished, he stepped back. "Bye, Lily." It took every ounce of his resolve to walk away. And he'd almost managed it when he heard her call his name. Aidan slowly turned and walked back toward her. They met in the middle.

"I—I know you were planning to stay in the city and I'll understand if you have things to do there. But—"

"But?"

"But…" She took a deep breath. "I'm all alone at the house, at least for the next week. And it's really nice. We have a pool and a tennis court and if you want, you're welcome to…join me."

"You're inviting me to the Hamptons?"

"Yes. And we have a guesthouse, too. Actually, it's the pool house, but you're welcome to stay there if you want more…privacy."

Hell, this had come out of left field. But Aidan wasn't about to give her time to change her mind. "Yeah, I'd like to come to the Hamptons with you, Lily Hart. I think we could have a really nice time."

She smiled, delight sparkling in her green eyes. "Good. What about your luggage?"

He pointed to the bag slung over his shoulder. "This is all I have," he lied. "I travel light, too."

Hell, he could do without the bag he'd checked. The airline would return it. And if he had to, he'd buy new clothes. He was going to the Hamptons with Lily Hart. In a limo. There was no predicting what might happen along the way. And once they got there, he planned to finish what they'd started on the plane.

3

THE MOMENT the driver shut the door behind them, Lily knew what would happen. It had been simmering beneath the surface from the moment they'd left the bathroom in the airplane. They were alone again, in their own little world, the tinted windows and privacy screen providing absolute isolation from reality.

Aidan's fingers tangled through the hair at her nape and he pulled her into a long, deep kiss.

The decision to invite him to the Hamptons had been made quickly and without much thought. It just seemed like the best thing to do. She didn't want to leave him at the airport, knowing they might not see each other again. And Miranda wasn't due to arrive for a week. She'd have the entire house to herself. The new and improved, wild and spontaneous Lily Hart didn't have to think twice about what she wanted.

His mouth trailed kisses to the curve of her neck and he groaned. "I guess you know what you're talking about."

"What do you mean?" Lily asked.

"You don't need ten minutes. You had me the minute that car door closed."

"I'm not trying to seduce you," Lily said, smiling as he breathed softly against her ear.

"You're not?"

"No, you're trying to seduce me."

Aidan pulled back. "I don't think so."

"You kissed me first."

"But I had to. I didn't have a choice."

Lily arched an eyebrow. "You always have choice."

"For someone who knows everything about seduction, you don't understand the male libido very well. It's nearly impossible for a man to resist when a woman is so…interested."

Lily gasped. Well, she'd managed to destroy any kind of mystery she'd acquired. Now he just thought she was easy. "All right, I'm not interested."

"I don't believe you," Aidan said, a smile curling the corners of his mouth.

Lily slid over to the other side of the seat and watched him warily. He relaxed, slipping out of his jacket and setting it between them. Her gaze drifted along his torso as she remembered the feel of his naked chest beneath her touch, the soft dusting of hair, the ripple of muscle across his abdomen.

She clutched her hands in her lap, noticing the trembling of her fingers. Why was she suddenly so nervous? The bathroom of a jetliner or the back of a limo, it didn't really matter, did it? They were both the stuff of sexy fantasies. But on the plane, Aidan was a stranger, a man who'd walk away once they landed. Now, he was a man on his way to the Hamptons—with her—and that was an entirely different matter.

He casually draped his arm across the back of the seat and toyed with a strand of her hair. A delicious shiver raced through her and Lily felt her heart flutter at his touch. "Nice limo," he murmured, glancing around.

"It is," she said, trying to ignore the pounding of her heart. "Though not as nice as some."

"Big backseat," he commented with a devilish grin.

Lily shrugged. "I'm sure it's big enough."

Aidan leaned closer. "So, tell me about this book you wrote. Ten seconds isn't very long. Are most men really that susceptible?"

"Ten minutes, not ten seconds. The title is a bit mis-leading," Lily explained. "It really means that a woman can attract a man in ten minutes. That something as simple as a glance or a touch can make a man want her."

"And what about men? What can I do in ten minutes to make a woman want me?"

Lily giggled. "Women aren't that easy. It takes a little longer." Although, he'd managed to attract her in about ten seconds. Lily drew a sharp breath, remember-ing that day, a year ago, when she'd first laid eyes on him.

He reached over and toyed with the buttons on the front of her blouse. As he opened each one, he drew the fabric back, exposing another inch of skin. "So, slowly removing your blouse, would that work?"

Lily moaned softly as he reached the last button and

pushed the fabric aside. Now that she wasn't in charge of the seduction, she wasn't sure what to do. Every touch, every sensation sent waves of desire coursing through her body. She didn't want to fight it. What did she have to lose, beyond her very last inhibition? "I think that would work."

He pressed a kiss between her breasts. "How about that? Kissing this soft spot right here. Is that working?"

Lily's head tipped back and she sighed as he cupped her breast in his hand. "Oh, that's nice."

"And what was that? Ten seconds? Maybe fifteen?"

She gasped, then tugged his hair until he looked into her eyes. He was entirely too sure of himself. Maybe it was time to make him work a little harder. "It's ten minutes, not ten seconds. And it only takes a half second for me to change my mind," she warned.

His arm snaked around her waist and he pulled her beneath him, then he kissed her, his tongue invading her mouth until she was forced to surrender. "And a half second to change it back."

This time, it was slow and easy between them. Clothing was no longer something to be disposed of quickly, but an enjoyable part of the foreplay. As the scenery rushed by outside the tinted windows, they undressed each other until Aidan was left in just his boxers and Lily in her underwear.

"Isn't this where we left off?" he asked, nibbling on her earlobe.

Lily moaned softly. "At least we won't have to worry about turbulence."

He slipped his hand beneath her bra and teased at her nipple. "But I am going to try to make the earth move again…if you don't mind."

This time, Lily's breath caught in her throat. "I—I just meant that—oh, that's nice—turbulence—it comes from the mixing of warm air with cool air and—" Lily cried out as his fingers slipped beneath the waist of her panties and found the damp spot between her legs. "Never mind," she murmured.

"No," Aidan said, raising his head to look into her eyes. "Tell me more."

"I don't think I can talk and…you know…"

"Not good at multitasking?"

Lily giggled. "No, it's just that—I prefer to focus my attentions on just one thing." Boldly, she reached down and rubbed her hand over the front of his boxers. He was already hard, his shaft warm beneath the soft cotton.

"If I had to pick one thing, that would be it," he said softly.

They continued to play, taking time and enjoying each new sensation. Outside, the countryside had given way to a small city, but Lily barely noticed. They stopped a few times and Aidan glanced up from his gentle exploration of her left nipple. "Ferry," he murmured.

"How long?" Lily asked, watching him through a haze of desire.

"I don't know. An hour. Maybe two." He sat up and pulled her half-naked body on top of his, her legs straddling his hips. "Plenty of time."

"People can't see in the windows, can they?" she asked.

"It's a bit late to start worrying about that." He kissed her neck. "No, they can't. There's a reflective finish on the outside. I checked before we got in." He glanced over to watch as a crew member from the ferry directed them onboard. The limo dipped as it drove across the clanging metal gangway and slipped between two cars.

"I feel like I'm naked in a public place," she murmured.

"Feels kind of naughty," Aidan teased.

Lily brushed aside her worries and pushed up on her knees as Aidan traced a line with his tongue over her belly. But when queasiness washed over her, Lily sat back down and closed her eyes. He nuzzled her neck and she drew a deep breath. The lack of sleep and the champagne for dinner had picked a bad time to take their toll.

"Oh," she murmured as her stomach lurched. She swallowed back the nausea, then realized it wasn't a hangover. It was the way the car was shifting back and forth beneath them. She'd felt this way before—whenever she was on a ship. "Stop. I don't feel so good."

Aidan drew back and frowned. "What's wrong?"

"I just feel really… Like I'm going to…"

"Here?"

Lily nodded. "I usually have to take medication. I just wasn't planning on any travel by ship. Maybe it's something I ate. Or drank."

"You get seasick?" he asked.

"Yes," she murmured, swallowing back a surge of

nausea. "Last summer, I took the *QE* II across the Atlantic. It was horrible. I was sick the whole way."

Aidan cursed beneath his breath, then grabbed her blouse and carefully pulled it over her arms. "Fresh air," he said. "That will make you feel better."

"Don't move!" Lily drew in another breath. "I—I think it would be best if you just left me alone."

He grabbed his pants and tugged them on, then slipped his feet into his flip-flops. By the time he'd pulled his shirt over his head, Lily was certain she was going to embarrass herself. But instead of leaving, Aidan helped her get dressed.

"I'm going to throw up on you," she warned.

"You'll do anything to drive me wild with desire, won't you?" he asked, a wry grin twitching at his mouth.

When she'd regained her modesty, Aidan opened up the door and stepped out, then reached inside to help her onto the rolling deck of the ferry. They were inside the cavernous auto deck, amongst the other cars. Lily looked back to see a huge hole in the rear of the boat where the cars had entered. Through it she saw the shore slowly retreating behind them.

She moaned, her knees buckling, and Aidan took her arm and helped her to the stairs. Slowly, they climbed to the upper deck, to sunlight and fresh air. Lily clutched at the rail while Aidan gently rubbed her back.

"Give me your arm," he said.

"Are you going to throw me overboard?"

"No." He took her wrist and pressed his fingers

against her inner arm just above her pulse point. "There's an acupressure point here. Sometimes it works, sometimes it doesn't." He rubbed her back with his free hand and before long, Lily began to relax.

"Better?"

Lily nodded, surprised that the nausea had retreated. First the turbulence and then the seasickness. She was beginning to get the feeling that the gods of sexual pleasure were conspiring against her.

"Maybe I should get you something to eat or drink?"

She shook her head. "I'm not sure that would help." Lily leaned her elbows on the railing and closed her eyes again. "Maybe some crackers?"

"I'll be right back," he said. "Just keep pressing on that spot."

Lily took another deep breath, and then another. After a few more minutes, she felt almost normal. When she straightened, she noticed a small group of passengers staring at her. Lily watched as a teenage boy approached, a hesitant smile pasted on his face.

"Is that Aidan Pierce?" he asked. "The guy you're with? I thought I recognized him."

"Do you know him?" Lily asked.

"Yeah. He directed *Halcyon Seven*. Everyone knows him. He's, like, the best director ever."

"That's what I've heard," Lily said.

"Do you think he'd mind if I took his picture? Or maybe got his autograph? My friends over there don't believe it's him."

Lily swallowed hard. "As long as I'm not in the

photo, I think it would be fine." Right now, between their romp in the car and the seasickness, she could only imagine what she looked like.

"Are you his wife?" the teen asked.

"No."

By the time Aidan returned, a group of five boys had gathered around her, babbling on and on about their favorite parts of Aidan's most popular film to date—a science-fiction film about a doomed space station. Lily had watched it twelve times, listening to the director's commentary on the DVD. Aidan patiently posed for a few photos and signed their T-shirts before he shooed them away.

"Sorry," he murmured.

"So I guess you're pretty famous," Lily said.

"Kind of. At least with teenage boys. *Halcyon Seven* was an adaptation of a graphic novel so a lot of diehard fans think it's the best out there. I don't really share that opinion. It was a job."

"I've never seen it," Lily lied. "You don't think it's good?"

He shook his head. "It was all right. But I don't want to be stuck in the action genre forever. There's just so much you can do with all those explosions and chase scenes. I want to work on the film that means something, that moves people emotionally." He glanced over at her. "That's why I haven't taken on any new projects. I'm going to wait for the right thing to come along."

"It must be flattering that they all want to meet you."

"Yeah, the fans are okay. It's the other people, the

people who want more than just an autograph. They can make it kind of difficult."

He handed her a bag of cheese crackers and a can of ginger ale. Then he reached in his pants pocket and pulled out a box of apple juice, a banana and a roll of Lifesavers. "I wasn't sure what would do the trick," he said.

"Let's start with the Lifesavers," she said.

He opened the candy, then picked through them until he found the red one. "Red is always better," he said.

"Thanks," Lily said. It was a silly gesture, but oddly thoughtful.

She glanced over at him, observing his profile in the morning sun. This had been the strangest encounter she'd ever shared with the opposite sex. She'd gone from the heights of passion to the depths of humiliation, all within the course of eight hours. But through it all, Aidan had been sweet and considerate and playful and sexy, exactly the kind of man a girl would want when it came to a casual fling.

But as she studied his handsome face, Lily realized that whatever this fling might have been to him, it didn't feel casual to her. It wasn't a fantasy anymore. It was real and wonderful and something that was growing more important with every moment she spent with him.

Lily closed her eyes. This was something she'd never bothered to cover in the book. Sure, it might be fun to seduce a man in ten minutes. But what happens an hour or two later, when you can't forget the feel of his hands on your body, or the scent of his cologne or the color of his eyes?

Well, she'd have an entire week to figure it all out. And maybe, once she'd gathered some more empirical data, she could start writing a sequel to her book. *After the Ten-Minute Seduction.* It might prove much more popular than the original.

AIDAN LEANED up against the back of the limo as he dialed Miranda Sinclair's phone number on his cell. She answered after three rings. "Hello, Aidan Pierce."

"Hi, Miranda. How are you?"

"Busy as always. I'm so sorry I had to cancel our meeting. Deadlines. You know how that goes. But I'm coming out to the Hamptons next week. Maybe you can take the train out from the city and we can have lunch then?"

"Actually, I'm going to be staying in the Hamptons with a friend. So, whenever you arrive, just give me a call. I'm really anxious to talk to you about the new book. I read the treatment and I think I could turn it into a great film."

"I think you could make it into one, too, darling. So, where are you staying? With anyone I know?"

"Actually, she's a writer. She writes under the name Lacey St. Claire, but her real name is Lily Hart. Her family has a house near Eastport. Isn't that where your house is?"

"There are so many people living in the Hamptons these days, I can't keep track of them all. I've never heard of the name. You'll have to introduce us."

"Maybe," Aidan said. "I'll talk to you next week, then." They said their goodbyes and Aidan switched off his phone, staring down at it for a long moment. He hadn't thought about where he and Lily might be in a week. In truth, he'd been living moment to moment since he'd stepped on board that plane.

But now that he'd had a chance to consider it, Aidan realized he wanted to believe they'd still be talking to each other, that they'd be making plans, that they might find something beyond their sexual relationship.

He'd never allowed himself to be optimistic about a woman before. Dating in Hollywood required a pretty cynical view of relationships. Aidan had known all along that he wasn't likely to find the love of his life in L.A.

His parents were still happily married after thirty-five years. He wanted to believe there was a future like that waiting for him, a happy ending. But he'd put that all on the back burner once he'd moved out west. And, in all honesty, he hadn't dated one woman whom he'd wanted to be with for more than a month or two.

It had given him quite a reputation around town, but strangely, attractive women found the challenge to be irresistible. He'd never quite understood what they'd seen in him, why they were willing to risk rejection just to say they'd dated him.

Aidan glanced up to see the driver walking toward the car. Lily was still inside the convenience store, buying something else to calm her stomach. Aidan slipped his phone into his pocket then gave him a wave. The driver took that as an invitation and quickly approached.

"Hey, I gotta tell you, Mr. Pierce, it's an honor to have you in my limo. I loved your last film. I've been a *Halcyon Seven* fan for years and you really did a great job on that movie. You stayed true to the fans, man." He held out his hand. "My name's Joe. Joe Roncalli."

Aidan reached out and shook his hand. "Thanks. I appreciate that. So, what is she doing in there?"

Joe shrugged his shoulders. "You're going to do a sequel, aren't you? *Halcyon Seven* was the best sci-fi movie made in the last ten years. You can't just leave the fans hanging."

"They haven't offered me a sequel," Aidan said. "And I'm thinking I really need to try something different. Something outside the action genre."

"Well…like what? Not one of those chick flicks. Man, I hate those movies."

"No. Maybe a thriller?" He glanced over at the store again. "I think I'll see what's taking Lily so long."

"I'm going to start a letter-writing campaign," Joe shouted after him. "Maybe even get an Internet petition together."

A few seconds later, Lily came hurrying out the front door of the store, a plastic bag dangling from her wrist. "I'm ready. We can go now." She smiled at him. "They have Krispy Kremes. And chocolate milk. I bought us some breakfast." She took a slug from the bottle of bright-pink antacid that she held in her hand. "Want some?"

Aidan shook his head. "I'll pass." Though dark circles colored the skin beneath her green eyes and her wavy hair was tousled, the color had returned to her cheeks. Aidan had to admit, she still looked sexy as hell, even in the bright light of day.

He'd touched her body, cupped the soft flesh of her breasts in his hands. He'd caressed her until she'd surrendered to him. And she'd made him ache with need. And here they were, the two of them, standing in the parking lot of a convenience store, two strangers who'd been far too intimate with each other already. He wasn't quite sure how to proceed.

"Do you have everything you need?" Aidan asked.

She nodded. "Do you know where you're going?" Lily asked, turning to the driver.

"I've got satellite navigation," Joe said. "Looks like it will be thirty or forty minutes."

They spent the rest of the drive chatting about places to see and things to do in the Hamptons. Aidan watched as she ate three donuts and then washed them down with a bottle of chocolate milk. He hadn't seen a woman eat that much since…well, he'd never seen a woman eat that much.

Her hunger sated, Lily leaned back in the seat and sent him a sideways glance. "When we get to the house, I'm going to take a long, hot shower and then a nap. Between the flight and then the ferry, I'm exhausted. And I probably look like death warmed over."

He reached out and smoothed her hair out of her eyes. "You look beautiful."

A pretty blush colored her cheeks and she leaned over and dropped a kiss on his lips. He caught her and a moment later, they were lost in something much deeper and more stirring. She tasted like sugar and chocolate milk.

He turned to face her, resting his head on the arm he'd stretched across the back of the seat. "Answer a question for me," he murmured.

"What do you want to know?"

"Why did you ask me to come with you? I mean, you could have just walked away. We would never have seen each other again."

Lily studied him for a long moment, her head tilted slightly. "I don't know," she said. "I just did. I...I couldn't seem to stop myself."

"You're kind of an impulsive person, then?" he said.

Her eyes went wide and she shook her head. "No, that's just it. I'm the least impulsive person in the world. I plan out everything. My life is so organized nothing ever surprises me." She paused. "You surprised me."

"I'd say it was the other way around. You surprised me."

"I think I like surprises," she said.

"So do I." He leaned forward, pressing her back into the soft leather seat. His lips found hers and he kissed her, slowly and thoroughly. It was nice not to have to worry about time. There was no ticking clock anymore. And though he wanted her more than he ever did, Aidan was willing to wait until they were completely comfortable.

"Why are you so organized?" he asked, trailing a line of kisses along the side of her neck.

She considered his question thoughtfully. At first,

Aidan wasn't sure that she was ready to reveal any-thing personal about her life. He braced his arm beside her and pushed up.

Lily glanced at him hesitantly, as if gauging how much she could say. Then she drew a deep breath and began. "There was a time in my life when everything was just—crazy. From one day to the next, I didn't know what was going to happen. I was young—twelve, thirteen. And the only way I could cope was to organize things. I'd go into my room and I'd organize my closet and organize my stuffed animals. I'd put all my CDs and books in alphabetical order and then I'd put them in chronological order. And when I was done, I'd re-arrange my closet again." She forced a smile. "I'm not obsessive-compulsive. I just was able to find comfort in organization. It distracted my mind."

"Why did you need comfort?" he asked.

"My parents were divorcing and I was caught in the middle. Actually, I wasn't really in the middle. More off to the—" She stopped short, biting her bottom lip. Her lips pressed into a tight smile and she shrugged. "Anyway, reading used to be my favorite thing to do, so when I went to college I decided to combine my two most favorite things—organization and reading. I majored in library science."

Aidan blinked, surprised by the sudden shift in con-versation. "You were a librarian?"

"No, not officially. You need a master's degree for that. But that's what I thought I wanted to be. I guess I'm still involved with books. Just in a different way."

"Have you written anything else, I mean, besides your seduction book?"

"Yes," she murmured.

He waited for her to expand on her answer and when she didn't, Aidan decided that he'd pushed her far enough. There was a reason she wasn't anxious to reveal more of herself than she had. He wasn't sure what it was, but he planned to find out.

Aidan ran his thumb along her lower lip. In such a short time, he'd come to appreciate the tiny details of her features—her lush mouth, her deep green eyes, the way her hair fell around her face. He couldn't get enough of touching her and looking at her.

"Why did you agree to come?" she asked.

"I guess I was intrigued," he said.

She seemed surprised by his admission. "By me?"

"Of course. Who else? You are the one who dragged me into the bathroom and had your way with me. I thought, if I stuck around, maybe I could have my way with you."

A blush crept up her cheeks. "I think that could be arranged. Once we're on solid ground."

The car slowed quickly, then stopped. Lily glanced up and smiled. "We're here. He missed the driveway."

A few seconds later, the driver backed the limo up and turned toward the gate. Lily rolled the privacy screen down and gave him the code and before long, they were winding down toward the water. When they pulled up in front of the house, Lily glanced over at Aidan.

"Nice," he said.

"Yes, it is nice."

The driver opened the door and helped Lily out, then went back to retrieve their bags from the trunk. He carried them up to the front door, then tipped his hat.

"It's been a pleasure driving you folks. You have a nice vacation. And I am gonna start that petition, Mr. Pierce, I promise."

Aidan clapped Joe on the shoulder. "Thanks."

He followed Lily into the house, carrying her bag along with his. Though the house was large, it wasn't as ostentatious as some of the mansions in the area. It was an older shingle-style "cottage," a sprawling two stories with high ceilings and plenty of windows.

When they got to the kitchen, Lily threw open a set of French doors and stepped outside. A wide veranda led to stone steps and then the pool. Just beyond it was a low, shingled building with a wall of doors facing the house.

She glanced back at him. "It's this way," she said.

He wondered why she'd chosen to give him separate accommodations when he was certain they'd be spending plenty of time in bed together. But then, maybe she had other plans. Though he was ready to pull her into the nearest bed, strip off her clothes and make love to her, Aidan decided to wait and take things a bit more slowly.

Maybe she was regretting her impulsive behavior. Or maybe she was wishing she hadn't invited him at all. But taking the time to seduce her properly would make the end result even more enjoyable.

LILY SAT in the center of her bed and stared down at her cell phone. She knew Miranda would be expecting her call. After all, she'd arranged for the limo, knowing that Lily would never want to get back on a plane after getting off. And she'd probably already calculated how long it would take to drive to the ferry, cross the Sound, and then arrive at the summer house. Drawing a deep breath, she pressed the memory dial key for the Beverly Hills house and waited for Miranda to pick up.

"Finally," Miranda said, not bothering with a greeting.

"I'm here, safe and sound. And thank you for the limo. I had a hard enough time with the first up-down, I'm not sure I could have handled another."

"How was your flight, darling?"

"Bumpy," Lily said. Though she wanted to tell Miranda every wonderful detail, she knew her godmother would have hours of advice to give and would call every hour to find out how things were going. It wasn't worth getting Miranda's hopes up if nothing came of this. "But I'm here."

"Maybe I should come out right away. I don't want you to have to be alone in that big house."

"No!" Lily paused, schooling her tone. "No, I'm fine. I'll have Luisa come in tomorrow and stock the fridge and do some cleaning. And it will give me a chance to relax, maybe get some sun. How is the book coming? Any progress?"

"Don't talk about the book," Miranda said. "It's a disaster. My worst one yet. I wouldn't be surprised if my publisher refuses to print it. I'll be forced to sell the houses and live in a box on the beach."

"You always say that and your books are always wonderful."

"Darling, I want you to go into town and arrange a book-signing for me at that little shop that I like so much. And arrange one for yourself, too. I talked to my editor today, and she said that the distributors are reporting good things. There are women out there who are buying it."

"Maybe I could buy a box next door to yours with my royalty check," Lily teased.

Lily heard a splash and crawled off the bed, the phone still pressed to her ear. When she got to the French doors at the far end of her bedroom, she pulled the sheer curtains back to see Aidan swimming laps in the pool.

The sun glistened on his back and she found herself focused on the way his shoulder muscles rippled as he moved through the water. "I—I have to go," Lily said.

"What? You can't talk to me a little longer?"

"No, Miranda, I'm really tired and I just need to sleep. I promise, I'll call you tomorrow." She switched off her phone before Miranda had a chance to protest any further.

Lily turned her attention back to Aidan, her gaze following him as he swam back and forth. He swam powerfully and efficiently, his arms slicing into the water with barely a splash. When he reached the end of the pool, he executed a perfect flip turn and started in the other direction. She counted ten laps before she stopped counting.

It was 2:00 p.m. eastern time, which meant 10:00 a.m. California time. They'd both been up over twenty-four hours, had had far too much to drink, and he still had the energy to swim laps. "Sexual frustration," she murmured. The words slipped out of her mouth before she realized she was thinking out loud.

Whatever it was, he'd worked it out. At the end of his next lap, he levered himself out of the pool and stood on the deck, dripping water. He shook his head, his shaggy hair tossing droplets of water into the air.

Her breath caught in her throat as she watched Aidan raise his arms above his head and stretch in the sun. His torso rippled and she clutched her hands together, her fingers aching to touch him again. She could just make out the trail of hair that marked his belly, knowing exactly what it led to.

Though she'd touched him, she hadn't had much chance to admire his body. He was tall, well over six feet, and finely muscled through his shoulders and arms. His waist and hips were narrow and he had beautiful legs, long and perfectly shaped for a man. "Nice calves," she murmured.

A shiver prickled her skin and Lily shook her head. An image flashed in her mind and she allowed herself to linger over it for a long moment. Aidan, naked, his body twisted in the pretty vanilla-and-pink striped sheets on her bed. What would it be like to have him for an entire night, to be able to enjoy his body some-where beyond the major modes of transportation?

Lily stepped back from the window, drawing a deep breath. She returned to the bed, trying to calm her nerves. She'd been so bold when they'd first met and now she was nothing more than a quivering mass of inse-curities. In this state, he'd see right through her. He'd know immediately she wasn't some sexy vixen with naughty intentions, that she wasn't worldly and experi-enced, the kind of woman who could attract any man.

Lily rolled off the bed and began to shed her clothes. When she was naked, she pulled open her bottom dresser drawer and searched for a swimsuit. She pulled out a turquoise-blue bikini she'd worn last summer, then tossed it aside for a more conservative one-piece.

But as she studied her reflection in the mirror, she realized that her figure really wasn't that bad. She exer-cised regularly, three times a week in Miranda's home gym, and she ate healthy meals and snacks prepared by Miranda's cook. Though she wasn't thin by Hollywood standards, she had enough on top and bottom to fill out a bikini.

She grabbed the turquoise suit from the floor. If she was going to do this, she was going to do it all the way, no inhibitions, no regrets, no one-piece swimming suits. She pulled on the bottoms, then slipped her head through the string that held the top together. Reaching back, Lily tied it, then reviewed the look.

"Not bad," she murmured. He'd seen her at her worst; it could only get better from now on. She wasn't panic-stricken, she wasn't nauseated and there were no fluorescent lights anywhere in the vicinity.

A soft knock sounded on the bedroom door. "Lily?"

His words were muted, as if he were afraid he might wake her from her nap. She hurried over to the door and pulled it open. Running her fingers through her hair, she pasted a bright smile on her face. "Hi," she said.

"I just wanted to check on you. See how you were feeling."

"I'm fine," Lily said. She watched as his gaze slowly drifted down her body.

"Wow," he murmured. "You look…almost naked."

It wasn't exactly a compliment, more a statement of fact. "Is that bad? I know I'm a little pale, especially by L.A. standards."

He reached out and slipped his hands around her waist, pulling her against his body. "Just don't expect me to keep my hands off you with all that exposed skin."

"I won't," Lily said, running her fingertips down his chest.

"I thought you were going to take a nap," he said.

"I thought I'd nap out by the pool and get some sun. You've been swimming?"

"Yeah," he said. "And now I'm starving. I was wondering if you knew of a place that might deliver lunch. Since we don't have a car and—"

"We have a car," Lily said. "And there's a deli in town that delivers. I can order some lunch for us."

"I'll order it. I owe you something for letting me stay here."

"We have an account. And there's no need to worry. You're a guest here. You don't owe me anything."

"I'm not used to being a kept man. I guess I'll have to work for my room and board in other ways."

"And how is that?" she asked, waiting for him drag her over to the bed. She could think of lots of ways to put his body to use.

"The pool really needs to be cleaned."

Lily blinked in surprise. "No, you don't have to do that. We have a pool man. He just doesn't come that often when we're not here."

"Well, come on down when you're ready. But don't put on sunscreen just yet. I can do that for you."

He gave her a quick kiss, his mouth lingering over hers for a long moment. Then he turned and walked back down the hall. Lily drew a ragged breath, placing her hand on her chest to feel her quickened heartbeat.

"I can do this," she said. "I can seduce this man again. I can make him want me."

She closed her eyes and repeated the words over and over again. She wasn't Lily Hart, unassuming research assistant, anymore. She was Lacey St. Claire, best-selling author and sex expert. And tonight, she'd have Aidan Pierce, naked, in her bed.

4

AIDAN LEANED back into the chaise and closed his eyes, tipping his face up to the sun. Though he lived in L.A. almost full-time now, he never really had a chance to appreciate the weather. He was always rushing from one meeting to the next, stuck in traffic or sitting inside a darkened office on a sunny day.

This felt good, to be outside in the sunshine. He'd spent the last two months in an editing suite. If he ever returned to L.A., he'd get rid of his house in the hills and buy a place on the beach, maybe in Malibu.

Squinting against the sun, he glanced over at Lily. She was stretched out on the chaise next to him, her eyes closed. "This is heaven," he said.

"Ummm," she replied.

"No planes, no boats, just this big, comfortable chair." He stretched his arms over his head and yawned. "I could really sleep right now."

She turned to him. "Then close your eyes and stop talking."

Aidan grinned. "But if I sleep now, I'll be all messed up for days. It's better just to stay awake." He swung his legs off the side of the chair. "Come on. If we swim, that will wake us up. Come in the water with me."

"I don't want to wake up," Lily groaned.

He straddled the end of her chaise and picked up her left foot to gently massage it. "You have such pretty feet."

"Oh, that feels good, slave boy." She giggled. "I'm sorry—slave assistant. Do the other one now."

Aidan dropped her foot, then crawled over her to brush his lips against hers. Her leg rubbed against his crotch as she shifted beneath him and the contact was like a shock to his system. He wanted to finish what they'd started earlier that day, right here, beside the pool. It was private enough.

"Come swimming with me." He nuzzled her neck. "You should always go swimming with a buddy. If you don't come with me, I might drown."

"If you need my help, just call." She smiled and closed her eyes.

Aidan pushed up from the chaise and walked over to the edge of the pool. He drew several deep breaths, then dove in, letting himself sink to the bottom of the deep end. As a kid, he'd always been able to hold his breath longer than anyone he knew. He sat on the bottom, staring up at the sky through the water.

He hadn't been on the bottom long when he saw Lily peering over the edge of the pool. She stepped back and Aidan slowly surfaced, floating to the top facedown like a corpse. An instant later, he felt a splash. Her arms wrapped around his waist and she dragged him into the shallow end of the pool.

But he twisted and grabbed her, pulling her along with him beneath the surface back into the deep end. When they bobbed back up, Lily coughed and sputtered and wiped the water from her eyes as he kept them afloat, their limbs tangled, their bodies pressed together.

"I—I thought you were drowning," she cried.

"I was just messing with you."

"You shouldn't do that!" she cried, slapping at him. "You scared me. I thought you'd hit your head."

"You saved me."

"I didn't want you to drown."

"You must like me, huh?"

She avoided his gaze, focusing on his chest instead. "Maybe I like you. A little."

Aidan pulled her into the shallow end again, and, when she could stand, he cupped her face in his hands and kissed her. Only this time it wasn't just a simple meeting of lips. He made his need for her quite clear. He plundered her mouth with his tongue until she sank against him, her body boneless and willing. Slowly, he drew back. "Do you really like me?" he teased. "Or do you just want my body?"

"I really like you," Lily murmured against his lips. "And I kinda like your body, too." She ran her fingertips along his collarbone. "Can we get out of this pool?"

"No more swimming?"

Lily shook her head, droplets of water sparkling on her lashes. "I think I've had enough sun for today."

Aidan grabbed her waist and lifted her out of the pool, setting her on the edge. Then he jumped out and helped her to her feet. His lips found hers again and as they stumbled toward the house, they didn't break the contact, lost in a flood of desire.

They left a trail of damp footprints from the kitchen to Lily's bedroom, the water still dripping from them as they tumbled onto her bed. Aidan brushed a strand of hair off her sunburned forehead. She sank back into the fluffy down pillows and closed her eyes, a smile curving the corners of her mouth.

He'd known her for less than a day and he'd spent most of their time together either taking care of her or trying to seduce her. It had become a bizarre relationship, if that's what it could be called. He wasn't sure exactly what was between them—acquaintance, a friendship? They weren't quite lovers, though he planned to change that as soon as possible. Right now, they were in between labels.

"Are you going to try to seduce me again?" he asked, dropping a line of kisses on her neck. "Because if you are, I'm not sure I'm going to be able to stop you. It might only take you three or four minutes, tops."

"And if I let you seduce me?" Lily asked. "How long do you think it would take?"

"I could seduce you in…ten hours."

Lily gasped. "Ten hours? You must be pretty bad if it takes you that long."

"No," Aidan said, with a devilish smile. "You don't understand. I'm that good. Give me ten hours and I guarantee you won't regret it."

"What time is it now?"

"Two o'clock. I'd have until midnight."

"I don't think it would take ten hours," Lily said. "More like ten minutes."

"Oh, I realize that," Aidan murmured. He smoothed his hands over her temples, pulling her hair back and looking directly into her eyes. "But think of all the fun we'll have taking it slow."

"And what if I resist? What if I don't want you after ten hours?"

"That won't happen," he said. "You'll want me. It's inevitable."

She drew a deep breath. "All right. I think we should get started right now. The clock is running. You can begin now."

Aidan lay down beside her and linked his arms behind his head. "So, I'm in charge?"

Lily nodded.

"Then I want you to stand up, right there, beside the bed."

She did as she was told, watching him warily. "Now what?"

"Take off that wet suit," he said.

She blinked, as if his request had taken her by surprise. But then, she slowly reached back and untied the strings that held the top on. A few seconds later, it dropped to the floor. Then Lily skimmed the bottoms over her hips and kicked them aside.

For a long moment, he let his eyes drift over her naked body. She kept her gaze fixed on his face, her breath coming in tiny gasps, her fingers trembling slightly.

"Do you have…you know—" She blushed. Lily couldn't even say the word *condom*. Someone who'd written a sex manual should at least be able to use the terminology.

"We won't need a condom," he said. "We're just going to take a nap."

She frowned. "Then I'm not sleeping with you if you're wearing those wet shorts," she said.

Aidan shimmied out of them, then patted the bed beside him. "Better?"

She nodded, then lay down. Aidan wrapped his arms around her waist and tucked her backside into his lap. His arms circled her body and he cupped her breast in his palm, lazily stroking her nipple with his thumb until it grew to a hard peak.

Her breath caught and then she let out a soft sigh. "We're just going to sleep?"

"Mmm-hmm," he said, kissing her shoulder. "Close your eyes."

"You're actually going to sleep?"

He drew a deep breath and smiled. Though he could have easily made love to her, Aidan liked the feeling of her body next to his in bed, of closing his eyes and knowing she'd be there when he woke up. He couldn't recall ever taking a nap with a woman. Hell, he didn't take naps. But right now, nothing seemed more appealing. "Your skin smells like coconuts," he whispered.

Lily twisted, looking over her shoulder at him. "This isn't my idea. Besides, I know how you're feeling." She pressed back against him, rubbing against his hard shaft.

Aidan stifled a moan. "We'll take care of that later," he said.

"I don't believe you. I think if I touched you, you'd feel compelled to do something. Men are very uncomplicated creatures."

"I'm just striking a blow for all men. Not all of us can be seduced in ten seconds. Now, close your eyes and go to sleep."

She turned over and faced him, then wrapped her arms around his neck and kissed him softly. "Ten minutes," she said.

This was crazy, to want her as much as he did. It was dangerous, addictive. He furrowed his fingers through her tangled hair, molding her mouth to his.

The soft flesh of her breasts pressed against his bare chest. God, she was so beautiful. Grabbing her leg, he pulled it up along his hip until his erection was nestled in between her legs. He was so close to the edge already, but he ignored the sensations racing through his body, willing himself to wait.

She nuzzled her face into his cheek and Aidan held his breath, wondering what it would cost him to resist her. But, after a few minutes, he realized that she wasn't going to push him any further. Her breathing had grown deep and regular. Lily was asleep.

Aidan closed his eyes and pulled her closer, inhaling the scent of her hair. This was a perfect way to spend the afternoon, the ocean breezes billowing the sheer curtains and the sound of seagulls in the distance. He'd wanted to get away from L.A., to find a place where he could clear his head. As far as he was concerned, he had found heaven.

THE ROOM was dark when Lily woke. She rolled over to find the other half of the bed empty, then rubbed her eyes. Aidan had covered her with a cotton blanket. She drew a deep breath of the salt-tinged air and smiled, snuggling into the warmth.

Lily had assumed this vacation would just be an endless stream of forgettable hours, the days running into nights, until Miranda arrived with more work to do. She had a stack of books left over from the previous summer she planned to read and she had research to keep her busy. And she'd planned to make a serious dent in the revisions on her novel. But now, all she wanted to think about was Aidan.

Raking her hands through her hair, Lily sat up, the blanket falling away from her naked breasts. She crawled out of bed and wandered over to the doors that opened onto the wide upper porch. The sun had set and the pool, though brightly lit, was empty.

She grabbed a simple cotton dress from the back of a chair and walked to the adjoining bathroom. When she turned on the lights, she was startled by the woman staring back at her from the mirror. Her hair, usually so carefully straightened every morning, was a riot of waves and curls. And her pale face was pink from the sun, a sprinkling of freckles dotting her nose and cheeks. She looked—different. Almost sexy. The kind of woman who might attract a man like Aidan Pierce.

Had they bumped into each other in L.A., he wouldn't have given her a second glance. A sliver of guilt pricked her conscience as Lily remembered the day she'd first seen him, over a year ago. Would the attraction have been there if Miranda had introduced them then?

Maybe the time had to be right. Maybe she just had to be ready. Or maybe she'd fantasized about him for so long that meeting him had become her destiny. Someday, she might tell him about her fantasies, about how he'd been her perfect man before they'd even met.

She smiled at her reflection. For the first time in her life, she believed she might find someone she could love forever. Not that she could love Aidan, they'd just met. But she'd never felt quite this way; every moment was filled with anticipation, and the very thought of him made her giddy with excitement.

Lily pulled the dress over her head, not bothering with underwear. The faded cotton felt good against her sunburned skin. When Aidan touched her again, she wanted as little between them as possible.

She decided to leave her hair wild and unruly and didn't bother with makeup. It was amazing how feeling good made her look so much better. The circles were gone from beneath her eyes and she couldn't stop smiling.

When she got downstairs, she found Aidan in the kitchen, sitting at the wide marble island. He was reading and didn't hear her enter. Lily watched him for a long moment, taking the time to appreciate just how gorgeous he was. He wore a loose white cotton shirt, unbuttoned to the waist, and a pair of comfortable khaki cargo shorts. His feet were bare and his hair uncombed. Their afternoon in the sun had burnished his skin a golden brown.

"What are you reading?" she asked.

He glanced up and smiled. "Nothing. Just a script. I was wondering if you were going to sleep the night away."

"You would have let me? What about your plan?"

He glanced at his watch. "Right now, my plan is dinner." He walked over to the refrigerator and grabbed a bowl, then set it on the counter.

"Did you make this?"

"No. I called that deli you mentioned. I found a menu next to the phone and they delivered about a half hour ago. Good thing I'm able to dial the phone. I'm not much of a cook. I survive on frozen pizza and takeout. And when I'm working on a movie, there's always catering."

He grabbed a pair of candles from the buffet in the breakfast nook and set them in front of her. Then he retrieved an open bottle of white wine and poured her a glass.

"Thanks," she murmured.

He stared at her for a long moment, then smiled. "You look beautiful."

"I got some sun."

Aidan leaned on the counter, bracing his elbows in front of him. "This is a nice place," he said, glancing around. "It feels like a home."

Lily nodded. "I like it. Although I wish it was just an easy train ride away from L.A."

"Did you and your parents come here when you were a kid?"

Lily shook her head and took a sip of her wine. "My parents have never been here."

"Oh, I thought you said it belonged to your family."

"It's a long, complicated story."

"Then answer an easy question. Am I the first guy you've ever brought here?"

"That one is much easier," Lily said. "Yes." She took a long sip of her wine. "I'm not really very good with men."

It was a difficult admission to make, but she didn't want to pretend anymore. She wasn't Lacey St. Claire. She didn't have any practical knowledge in the art of seduction. She was going to make love to Aidan, and she wanted him to make love to her—Lily Hart—not an illusion she'd created.

"I kind of got that," he said.

"You did?"

Aidan nodded. "So, why the book?"

"I guess it was an exercise, a way to learn a little more. It was a silly project and I didn't think it would go anywhere. It wasn't even my idea." She drew a deep breath. "I had a boyfriend. A year and a half ago. His name was George. I thought maybe we might get married someday. But then, he told me I wasn't sexy enough."

Aidan laughed out loud. "Well, George was an idiot."

"No. He just wanted someone…better…you know,

a blonde, with a big chest…and long legs. All men think that's sexy."

"I don't," Aidan said as he filled a plate with salad.

"But you dated—" Lily stopped herself. She could list all the beautiful women Aidan had dated, blondes and otherwise. They were all documented in the celebrity magazines.

"Yeah, I've dated girls like that. It doesn't take much to look like everyone else. It takes much more to be an original."

"Am I an original?"

He handed her the salad. "Oh, yes. You are definitely one of a kind, Lily Hart. I don't think I've ever met a woman quite like you."

They shared another bottle of wine with dinner and as they chatted about inconsequential subjects, Lily began to realize how subtle seduction could be. Every now and then, Aidan would touch her, in a seemingly innocent way, and she'd feel her pulse leap.

But he was also seducing her with his words, weaving a spell around her until she felt as if she were the most important woman in the world to him. He never took his eyes off her.

And yet, it didn't seem as though he was trying to make her want him. It all came so naturally that Lily had to wonder if perhaps Aidan had feelings for her. She knew she was risking her own heart by believing that, but she didn't care. Even if she was deluding herself, it was such a wonderful delusion, she just wanted to enjoy it while it lasted.

If he walked out of her life tomorrow, she'd have no regrets. A fantasy had come to life for her. How could that possibly be a bad thing?

Until now, Lily had watched life from the sidelines. What had she been so afraid of? She knew her parents' divorce had left some pretty deep scars, but she was an adult, and the scars should have faded long ago. For the first time in her life, she'd taken a real risk and the reward had been this man—this wonderful, funny, sexy man with the incredible blue eyes and the sculpted mouth. This man who wanted her as much as she wanted him.

Lily grabbed her glass of wine and gulped the rest down. Warmth pulsed through her veins and she felt a bit dizzy. Though she could appreciate this long, slow seduction, she was desperate to kiss Aidan.

Lily fixed her gaze on his lips and it took him only a moment to notice. "What are you doing?" he asked.

"I'm trying to get you to kiss me," she said.

"You could always get up, walk over here and kiss me," he suggested.

"Would that be against the rules?" she asked, slowly standing.

"There are no rules. Just a schedule." He looked at his watch. "A kiss would be right on time."

Lily sat down again and shook her head. Was she that predictable? "Hmm. I guess the urge passed. I don't need to kiss you anymore."

He slipped off the stool and pulled her to her feet. "Come on."

They wandered outside, strolling past the pool house and the bubbling whirlpool to the walkway that led down to the water. The moon was rising above Fire Island, creating a silver path of light that seemed to lead right to them. It was an impossibly romantic scene and Lily had to wonder if the moonrise was just a natural occurrence or part of Aidan's grand ten-hour plan.

"Did you order that moon?" she teased.

"Yeah," he said. "Just for you."

"You're good, I'll give you credit."

"You haven't even seen my best moves yet." He stood behind her with his arms around her waist and his chin resting on her shoulder. When he pressed a kiss to her neck, Lily moaned softly. He was barely trying and already she wanted to rip her clothes off and have her way with him.

She slowly turned in his arms to face him, her heart slamming in her chest. She could change the face of the game they were playing right now. Gathering her courage, Lily reached down and grabbed the hem of her dress, then pulled it over her head. It dropped out of her fingers and fell to the walkway.

"Now, that was a move," he murmured. Aidan pulled her body against his, his hands spread across the small of her back. The kiss they shared was deep and powerful, full of pent-up passion and the promise of so much more. His fingers danced over her skin, as if he couldn't get enough of her.

When he drew back to look down at her, Lily slowly

pushed his shirt off his shoulders. The planes and angles of his body gleamed in the moonlight and for a moment, Lily thought this all might be a dream. It was too perfect. And yet it was too real to be a fantasy.

She reached down to unbutton his pants and they slid down over his hips. He'd decided against underwear as well. He grabbed her hand and led her back to the whirlpool.

Until the airplane bathroom at twenty thousand feet, Lily had never experienced anything but ordinary sex. She knew, from all the magazines and books, that people had sex in all sorts of interesting locales, but she'd never moved beyond the front door of her apartment.

Aidan stepped down into the bubbling water, then turned to help her descend the stairs. When they were both up to their waists, he floated back, drawing her into his arms.

The sensation of his naked body brushing against hers was so tantalizing that for a moment, Lily lost herself in a dizzy rush. Though she wasn't the expert she pretended to be, she realized all she really had to do was react, without fear or inhibition. She'd be fine if she just let instinct take over.

His hands were all over her, her skin slick against his palms. Lily arched above him and he fixed his mouth on her nipple. Desire shot through her body like an electric shock and a cry of surprise slipped from her throat.

He took his time, exploring her body while the water

kept them weightless. Steam rose up around them as the night air began to chill, creating a cocoon, a separate world where there was just his touch and his taste, the sound of her name on his lips. And just when she thought it couldn't get better, he'd find a new way to tempt her desire.

Lily didn't remember making a conscious effort to return his caresses, it simply happened. She needed to feel his body beneath her fingers, to trace a path across his skin as if she were mapping out every inch of his body. When she slid down into the water and pressed her mouth to the center of his chest, Aidan braced his arms on the edge of the whirlpool and let her explore his body.

She got lost in the details, in the trail of hair on his chest, in the notch at the base of his throat, in the feel of his nipple beneath her lips. Slowly, she found her favorite spots and lingered there. He watched her through half-closed eyes, his expression intense. And when she let her hand drift below the surface of the water, he held his breath.

Her fingers closed around his shaft and a smile curved the corners of Aidan's mouth. She watched his face as she stroked, his reactions dancing across his expression, shifting with each caress. He moaned softly as she increased her tempo and then suddenly grabbed her hand to stop her.

Wrapping his hands around her waist, Aidan lifted her from the whirlpool and set her on the side. He pressed his palm against her chest, slowly sliding it down until she leaned back on her elbows. Lily knew what he was about to do, but she wasn't prepared for how it would feel.

His mouth was warm, his tongue finding the spot immediately. The chilly breeze prickled goose bumps on her skin, but Lily didn't feel the cold. All she could focus on was the way his mouth teased at her sex. She tried to relax and let go, but she wasn't sure she'd be able to control herself once she did. Pleasure had never come naturally to her, yet now it seemed as though it was rushing over her like a waterfall, everything that she'd missed coming on full-force.

Her pulse raced, her fingertips tingled and she shifted against his mouth. Suddenly, she was there, on the edge, teetering toward release. Lily's breath caught in her throat and she felt a sliver of fear.

She was surrendering a part of her soul to this man. This wasn't casual sex, this was liberation. She was discovering a part of her that she didn't know existed. Lily relaxed and let him take control again. A moment later, she dissolved into shattering spasms of pleasure. Her fingers tangled in his damp hair, drawing him close, then pushing him away as he tormented her with his tongue.

Fireworks went off in the sky above her head, blue and pink trails of light streaming down from the sky. She closed her eyes and her orgasm seemed to go on forever. When Lily finally floated back to reality, she was completely spent, boneless and dizzy. Aidan pulled her back down into the water and the warmth enveloped her. His lips found hers again and he kissed her, this time tenderly, her face cupped in his hands.

"You okay?" he asked, smoothing her hair back from her face and staring into her eyes.

"I think so." Another round of fireworks went off and Lily frowned. "Can you see those?"

He nodded. "Somebody must be celebrating the Fourth a few weeks early."

"Oh, good. They are real. For a minute there I thought they were—" Lily smiled wanly. "Never mind."

She wanted to tell him how incredible she felt, how wonderful he was, but Lily didn't want to admit that everything that she'd experienced with men up until him had been less that earth-shattering. *Thank you* just didn't seem appropriate at the moment.

THEY TUMBLED onto his bed in a tangle of naked limbs. Though Aidan had promised Lily a long, slow seduction, he'd grown tired of waiting. The woman in his arms had possessed him, body and soul, and now he wanted to possess her.

He'd never felt this kind of need before. Every nerve in his body ached to be touched by her. He craved the scent of her skin and the feel of her hair between his fingers. His self-control had vanished and in its place was an undeniable force driving him mad with desire.

Her body lay beneath his, Aidan taking his weight on his braced arms. His shaft, hard and hot, pressed against the soft flesh of her belly. With every caress, he felt himself losing touch with reality, slipping into a haze of passion. But this time, with Lily, he wanted to be aware of every single moment. If this ended in a week or two, he wanted to remember it all.

They barely knew each other; in truth, they were strangers. But there was something about Lily he could trust. As hard as he searched, he couldn't find an agenda or an ulterior motive.

He rolled over, pulling her along with him. When she was settled on top of him, Aidan slowly skimmed his palms over her torso. She had a woman's body, soft and curvy, not muscled and bony like so many women in L.A. She was completely natural…real. And so everything they did, everything he felt, seemed more real, as well.

"Are we going to do this?" he murmured.

Lily smiled. "I'm not sure."

He froze. "You're not—"

"No, I am," she quickly said. "It's just that every time we get here, something happens. I'm just waiting for the earthquake or the tidal wave. Or maybe a convenient tornado."

"I think we're safe," Aidan said.

The doors to the pool house were open and he could hear the pop of fireworks outside. He closed his eyes as Lily kissed him, the taste of her like a narcotic. Slowly, her lips trailed along his shoulder, then down the middle of his chest. The anticipation was excruciating, but Aidan waited, enjoying the sweet sensations coursing through his body.

When her lips closed around his shaft, all the breath left his body. He clutched at the sheets, twisting them through his fingers as he focused on something other than what Lily was doing to him. But it was no use. He was lost.

"Oh, Lily," he murmured, his fingers moving to her hair. "The things you do to me. They ought to be illegal." He twisted beneath her, then when he could take no more, he gently drew her away. Aidan grabbed a condom from the bedside table and handed it to her.

"I don't know if I can do this," she said, staring at the package. "It hasn't been ten hours."

Aidan chuckled. "It will be by the time we're finished." Two hours of making love to Lily didn't sound like enough, but he was certain that neither one of them would turn into a pumpkin at the stroke of midnight.

She took her time sheathing him and when she was finished, he pulled her down beside him and drew her leg up over his hip. Slowly, he entered her, biting down on his bottom lip as he slipped into her warmth. Aidan drew a ragged breath, his gaze still fixed on her face. A tiny moan slipped from her throat and he froze, but then she looked at him, her eyes meeting his. She shifted until he was deep inside her.

For a long time, they didn't move, just stared at each other, his fingers smoothing over her face, her palm pressed against his heart. He wasn't sure he'd ever felt such a deep connection before. How was that possible? He barely knew Lily.

They played at this slow seduction for a long time, Aidan moving inside her and then stopping as he explored her body with his lips and fingers. He was amazed at how closely he danced to the edge before pulling back. But with each position they tried, the need grew more acute and Lily more impatient.

He pushed up until he knelt between her legs, her thighs resting on top of his. He touched the damp spot between her legs, rubbing softly until she closed her eyes and arched her back. Aidan knew he wouldn't be able to last through her orgasm, but he didn't care. He began to move inside her and he watched as her fingers clutched the sheets.

When they came close, he slowed his pace, but it wasn't long before he reached the point of no return. Aidan knew she was ready when he felt her tighten around him. And then, a heartbeat later, she cried out, dissolving into spasms of pleasure.

It was too exquisite to deny, and he let himself go, surrendering to the feel of her body convulsing around his shaft. His release had been such a long time coming that it seemed to go on forever, powerful and mind-numbing.

By the time rational thought returned and he opened his eyes, she was staring up at him, a satisfied smile curving her lush lips.

Aidan raked his hands through his hair and grinned. "What?"

"I can't believe we actually did it," she said. "I half expected a meteor to come crashing through the ceiling."

"I did feel the earth move a little bit."

Lily reached up and traced his bottom lip with her fingertip. "Just a little bit?"

"All right. The tectonic plates shifted."

"Tectonic plates usually only move ten to forty milli- meters a year." She paused. "But then there are the occa- sional earthquakes. You were definitely an earthquake."

"How is it you know all these little facts?" Aidan asked.

"I just do. I remember everything I read. When I was younger, I didn't read books, I devoured them. Every few days, I'd go to the library and bring home stacks of things to read. I'd close myself in my room and escape into all of these perfect little worlds."

Suddenly, the last of Lily's walls were gone. He could see it in her eyes—complete vulnerability. It was what he truly wanted from her, yet it scared him a little. "That's how I felt about films," Aidan said. "When I went to the movies, anything was possible. Life was an adventure. I always thought it would be cool to be in charge of creating that world on the screen, of making it come alive. Both my mom and dad loved the movies. We used to go once a week, my whole family."

"That sounds so nice. You must have such nice memories of that. My parents never really did anything with me. I was always just…there, standing on the side- lines, watching their lives. I think a family is supposed to revolve around the kids, isn't it?"

"Were they divorced?" Aidan asked.

Lily didn't hesitate at all. What had happened between them had been deeply intimate. She was ready to trust him with who she really was. "It's not a happy story," she said. "They divorced when I was thirteen. My father moved to France and bought a vineyard. My mother took up with a series of Italian millionaires and she lives…well, she lives in a lot of different places, but mostly in a palazzo outside of Milan."

"That must have been interesting, living in Europe."

"I never lived with them after the divorce. I stayed in California to finish out the school year and moved in with my godmother. When summer rolled around, they were both too busy to take me, so I just stayed where I was. After that, I guess they figured I was happier without them."

Aidan felt his heart ache for Lily. He'd grown up in such a happy home. "I'm sorry. We don't have to talk about this."

"No, it's good," she said. "I've never really talked about it."

"Did you have any siblings?"

"No," Lily said. "I was an only child. I was kind of like an accessory to my parents' marriage. My mother was an actress and my father was a director. I guess they thought it would be good publicity to have a child, you know, a baby they could be photographed with. I suppose I'm lucky they didn't decide on a dog instead, or I wouldn't be here."

"Hart," Aidan murmured. "Was your father Jackson Hart?"

Lily nodded. "That's him. Dear old Dad."

"Then your mother must have been—"

"Serena Frasier."

Aidan gasped. "My God, Lily. You look just like her. There was something about you I recognized and that must be it. She was beautiful, your mother."

"She still is. You'd be surprised how having a rich husband keeps her looking young."

"And your father was a great director. We studied his film *Paper Trail* in film school."

"Everybody loved my parents," she said. "Especially the press. Every affair, every fight, every public reconciliation. I was there for all of it. I had a front-row seat."

"And you survived," Aidan said, drawing her more tightly into his embrace. If his touch could wipe away the pain he'd heard in her words, then he'd do his best. "You're a very strong woman, Lily."

"No," she murmured. "Not so strong."

She snuggled up against him and before long, was sound asleep. But Aidan continued to lie awake, his head filled with questions.

He'd lived in L.A. long enough to know that showbiz relationships were almost impossible. No one lasted forever anymore, not like his parents. Aidan had just taken it for granted he would never have something like that, something forever. But maybe there was someone in the world that belonged with him, someone so perfect they just—fit.

He nuzzled his face into Lily's hair and drew a deep breath. Lily fit pretty damn well. But she came with a history that had to make her wary of long-term relationships.

Aidan stared at the ceiling of the pool house, watching the reflected light from the water shimmer above him. This was crazy. He'd known Lily for twenty-four hours. How could he possibly be thinking about a future with her?

He closed his eyes and tried to relax. Nothing needed to be decided tonight. He had a week with Lily, seven days to figure out why he found her so fascinating. And he planned to use every minute of every day.

5

LILY RUBBED her eyes as she stared at the computer screen. Stretching her arms above her head, she tried to wake her body up. But it was no use without coffee.

She'd woken up an hour ago in Aidan's bed and found herself unable to go back to sleep. She wasn't quite sure about the protocol. Aidan had mentioned he never spent the night with his lovers, and she didn't want to make it uncomfortable for him, so she slipped out of bed.

She'd retrieved their clothes, discarded on the plank walkway, and pulled her dress over her head as she'd walked back to the house. A search for coffee in the kitchen proved fruitless. Usually Luisa, Miranda's Eastport housekeeper, took care of the shopping, but Lily had deliberately avoided calling her, knowing that Luisa would report back to Miranda about the strange man living in the pool house.

Lily smiled to herself. Not so strange. The sexy man. Her thoughts drifted back to the night before, to the long, slow seduction that Aidan had promised. It was everything she could have ever wanted, romantic and playful and electric. There were parts of her fantasy that she'd always left empty and now she knew why. The fantasy never could have lived up to the reality of making love to Aidan.

Love. It was such a big word. Though calling what they had shared *sex* was probably more to the point, Lily sensed there was something else between them, something deeper.

She drew a ragged breath and closed her eyes. Or perhaps he was just an expert at making her feel that way. Maybe that was all part of the seduction. If she expected to survive a week with Aidan, then she'd need to put their "activities" in perspective. Men needed to have sex. It was a biological imperative, and, unlike women, they usually didn't need to feel any deep level of emotional attachment in order to perform. It was all there in her book.

"Miss Lily?"

The sound of a voice startled her, and she spun around in the chair to find Luisa standing in the doorway. Pressing her hand to her heart, Lily forced a smile. "Oh, you scared me!"

The housekeeper gave her an apologetic look. "I'm sorry. That's why I thought I should tell you I was here. I didn't want to scare you."

"What are you doing here?"

"Miss Miranda called me to ask if I'd arrange to have the car tuned up before she arrived. I was surprised you were here on your own. I thought when she canceled her trip, you'd stay in California with her."

"No, I decided to come out early."

"Can I get you some coffee? I stopped at the market in town and picked up your favorite blend. There's a pot brewing right now."

"That would be wonderful," Lily said, yawning.

Luisa turned to leave, but Lily stopped her, calling her name. "Wait a second. There's something I need to tell you. We have a houseguest. His name is Aidan. Aidan Pierce. He's staying in the pool house."

"Would he like some coffee, too?" Luisa asked.

"No," Lily said, giggling softly. "He's still asleep. But I'd appreciate it if you wouldn't say anything to Miranda when she calls. You know how she can get and I just don't want to deal with her questions right now."

"Oh," Luisa murmured. "I understand. He's your guest. A special guest."

Lily paused. "I know your first loyalty is to Miranda and I don't want to put you in the middle of this. I won't be upset if you say something, but—"

Luisa held up her hand. "Don't worry, Miss Lily. I won't say a word. I understand there are times when you need your privacy. Let me know when you and Mr. Aidan would like breakfast. I've brought croissants from the bakery and strawberry jam from the farmer's market."

Lily crawled out of her chair and crossed the room, then threw her arms around Luisa, giving her a fierce hug. "Thank you."

She went back to her work, relieved that she wouldn't have to deal with Miranda for at least a few days more. It wasn't that she wanted to deliberately exclude the only person in the world who'd ever really cared about her. But everything that was happening with Aidan was so new and uncertain. She wanted to protect it from close examination for just a little while longer.

Common sense would say that there could never be anything lasting between them. She'd seen what her father's career had done to his marriage. And her mother hadn't helped. Making movies might be glamorous, but living on location was too tempting for any man or woman.

What happens on location, stays on location. That's what everyone said these days. But back when her parents were married, on-set affairs were considered off-limits. If affairs had been an accepted part of Hollywood life, maybe her parents might still be married.

But even if it was considered acceptable, could she really live that kind of life, wondering if the man she loved was temporarily loving someone else? It was impossible to imagine sharing a man like Aidan with any other woman—especially a beautiful movie star.

Lily turned back to the computer and scrolled through the two pages she'd rewritten. She worked on her novel whenever she found a spare moment, but it was still months from completion. There were days when she felt as if it would never be finished. But this morning, she'd found a new sense of confidence in her work.

She and Aidan had spent one night in the same bed and suddenly, Lily felt as if she could conquer the

NO POSTAGE
NECESSARY
IF MAILED
IN THE
UNITED STATES

BUSINESS REPLY MAIL

FIRST-CLASS MAIL   PERMIT NO. 717   BUFFALO, NY

POSTAGE WILL BE PAID BY ADDRESSEE

HARLEQUIN READER SERVICE
3010 WALDEN AVE
PO BOX 1867
BUFFALO NY 14240-9952

Play the Lucky Hearts Game

and get...

2 FREE BOOKS and
2 FREE MYSTERY GIFTS...
YOURS to KEEP!

yes! I have scratched off the silver card. Please send me my *2 FREE BOOKS* and *2 FREE mystery GIFTS* (gifts are worth about $10). I understand that I am under no obligation to purchase any books as explained on the back of this card.

Scratch Here!

then look below to see what your cards get you... 2 Free Books & 2 Free Mystery Gifts!

351 HDL ESTM   151 HDL ESWX

FIRST NAME   LAST NAME

ADDRESS

APT.#   CITY

STATE/PROV.   ZIP/POSTAL CODE   (H-B-07/08)

Twenty-one gets you
**2 FREE BOOKS and
2 FREE MYSTERY GIFTS!**

Twenty gets you
2 FREE BOOKS!

Nineteen gets you
1 FREE BOOK!

TRY AGAIN!

world. Yes, the sex had been incredible, but it didn't mean that her whole life was about to change.

"Get a grip," she muttered.

"Hey."

The sound of his voice sent a flood of warmth through her veins. Her pulse quickened and she closed her eyes and drew a deep breath, before turning in the chair. He wore the shorts he'd worn for most of the day yesterday. His chest and feet were bare and his hair tousled by sleep.

"Morning," she said.

He held up a mug of coffee, then crossed the room and set it on the desk. "The housekeeper said I should bring you this."

"Luisa," she said.

"I woke up and you weren't there," he murmured, taking a sip from his own mug of coffee. "The first time I actually spend an entire night with a woman and I end up alone in bed in the morning." He paused. "I guess I know how that feels now." Aidan glanced around. "So what are you doing in here?"

"Getting some work done."

"Nice office. Comfortable."

"Yes," Lily said.

She didn't quite know what to say to him. Was she supposed to thank him for the wonderful time in bed? She wanted to crawl out of her chair and throw herself into his arms and kiss him. But she couldn't get herself to move.

Aidan stepped over to the bookcases and peered at

the titles there. "You're welcome to take anything that looks interesting," she ventured.

"Thanks," he murmured. He moved over to the shelves that contained some of Miranda's awards. "Wow, are these all—" His voice died in his throat as he picked up a plaque and examined it carefully. "What are these? What are you doing with Miranda Sinclair's stuff?"

"She's my godmother," Lily said.

He stared at her, Miranda's plaque clutched in his hands. "What?"

"She's my godmother. This is her house."

"You said this was your family's house."

Lily shifted uneasily. She didn't like the tone of his voice or the way he was looking at her. "Miranda is my family. She took me in after my parents' divorce. I live with her in Beverly Hills."

A low groan slipped from his throat. "Oh, shit," he muttered. "Why didn't you tell me?"

"Tell you what?"

Aidan set the plaque back on the shelf. "And I was so careful with this. I mean, I never, ever mix business with pleasure." He shook his head, raking his fingers through his hair. "You were sitting in her seat. I was supposed to meet with her on the plane to discuss turning her new book into a movie."

His words hit her like a sharp slap to the face. Was this yet another one of Miranda's attempts at matchmaking? Miranda worked with a production company in Hollywood. She rarely had anything to do with the movie adaptations of her novels. And Lily had thought it a bit odd that Miranda insisted she go to the Hamptons alone. They always traveled together.

"I thought you said you were a writer," he murmured.

"I—I am. I also help Miranda with her research. It was her idea to do the seduction book and then I ended up writing the whole thing." Lily groaned, then covered her face with her hands. "I'm so sorry. Sometimes she just goes too far. She had no right to get you mixed up in this."

"What are you talking about? I'm the one who screwed up here. If she ever finds out we're sleeping together, she'll never want to do a project with me."

"She'd be thrilled if she found out we were sleeping together!" Lily cried. "At least I'd be sleeping with someone. If she knows it's you, she'll let you make her next *ten* novels into movies."

Aidan looked at her as if she'd just lost her mind. "What *are* you talking about?"

Lily stood, shoving the chair back from the desk. "Be honest. If you had known I was Miranda's goddaughter, would you have gone into that bathroom with me?"

Aidan took a moment to consider her question, but it seemed like a lifetime to Lily. She closed her eyes, preparing herself for the truth. When he drew in a sharp breath, she looked at him and he smiled crookedly. "Yeah. I would have. I'll find another project. It's no big deal."

Lily swallowed hard, unable to believe what she was hearing. "Really?"

He nodded, then circled the desk and pulled her into his arms. "Hey. There are plenty of things I can do." He tipped her chin up and kissed her softly, his hands smoothing over her hips to rest on her backside. "You really think Miranda would be happy that we're sleeping together?"

"Miranda likes to mess with my life," Lily said. "She thinks she knows what's best for me. That's why she made me write that book. She thought it would be good for me."

"So you're not really an expert on seduction?"

"On paper," she admitted. "But I don't have a lot of practical experience."

"Well, maybe we're going to have to work on that a little more," he whispered. "We could call it research. I could probably teach you a few things. And then you could teach me a few things. We could study together."

Lily sighed. "I didn't mean to make you believe I was something I wasn't."

"I guess we all pretend a little bit." He shrugged. "We could have spent the whole flight ignoring each other. Where would we have been then?"

"Not here."

"My point exactly."

As long as they were being honest, Lily knew she ought to tell him the whole truth, about the day she'd seen him at the airport, about how she'd harbored a secret crush on him for over a year. But there had to be limits to a woman's honesty. Or maybe she'd consider this an attempt to maintain at least a shred of mystery.

"Why don't you go ask Luisa to make us some breakfast? I need to call Miranda."

"It's 4:00 a.m. in California," he said.

"I know," Lily replied. "But it's never too early for a little payback."

He dropped a kiss on her lips. "Tell her thanks from me. And tell her I'm sorry we won't have a chance to work together."

Lily watched him walk out of the office, her thoughts spinning. Though his project with Miranda was probably never going to pan out anyway, it was nice to know he would have given it up for her. Though she didn't want to read too much into the gesture, it made her feel good to be chosen first.

Grabbing the phone, Lily flopped back down in the chair and kicked her feet up on Miranda's desk. She punched in the number for Miranda's landline, knowing the phone beside her bed would ring.

It rang five times before Miranda picked up. Lily heard a sleepy voice on the other end of the line. "Hello?"

"Miranda? Did I wake you?" She didn't wait for a response. "I just couldn't wait to tell you. I mean, I suppose I could have waited a few hours, but this is just too important."

"Lily? Is that you?"

"Miranda? I'm getting married. I'm in love. I know it's kind of spur-of-the-moment, but you're always telling me to be more spontaneous. And we're in love. I mean, we've only known each other for a day, but we knew right away. I know we can make it work. A lot of people do."

"Lily?"

"I have to go, Miranda. Thank you so much for everything. I know you want me to be happy and I am." Lily giggled to herself. If there was a way to get back at Miranda for her meddling, waking her up at 4:00 a.m. was a good start. And the rest, she'd have to live with for a few more hours.

Lily left the phone on and set the receiver inside a desk drawer. If Miranda tried to call back, her call would go through to voice mail. And if she tried to call Lily's cell phone, she just wouldn't answer.

When she strolled into the kitchen, she found Aidan perched on a stool at the counter, yesterday's copy of the *New York Times* spread out in front of him. Luisa was busy at the stove, making French toast. Lily grabbed a croissant from the basket in front of Aidan and sat down next to him.

"Did you get hold of Miranda?" he asked.

She popped a bit of the croissant into her mouth and nodded. "Yeah. Luisa, if Miranda calls on your cell phone, don't answer."

Luisa glanced over her shoulder. "And why would I do that?"

"Just as a favor for me. Just for a few hours." She turned to Aidan. "She might try to call you, too. Don't answer."

Aidan gave her an odd look. "All right."

Satisfied, Lily reached out and grabbed the book section from the *Times*. "Luisa makes the best French toast. Do we have any of those little sausages you get from the farmer's market?"

Aidan reached out and took her hand, lacing his fingers through hers. He brought her wrist up to his lips, pressing a kiss to the skin on the back of her hand. She gave him a sideways glance and smiled.

"I like this," she said. "Having breakfast together."

"So do I," he replied.

AIDAN STRETCHED out on his bed, the expensive sheets soft on his bare skin. Lily lay beside him, a satisfied smile on her face. "We are too lazy," she said, her fingertips running up and down his belly.

They'd eaten breakfast and then gone right back to bed, making love before falling asleep again. This was his idea of a real vacation. What more could a man want? A soft bed, a beautiful woman interested in pleasing him and a place where he could be comfortably naked for most of the day. All that was needed to make it really perfect was beer on tap and a big-screen television.

"How did I do?" Lily asked.

"I'll give you an A," he replied.

She turned toward him and gently bit his arm, grazing her teeth over his skin. He'd taught her what he liked, that mixture of pleasure with a little pain, and she'd taken the lesson seriously. She'd taught him that there were some women who found a long, leisurely foot massage extremely erotic. He'd never sucked on a woman's toes before, but Lily had seemed to enjoy it immensely.

"I'm giving you a B minus," she said.

"What? Why? I thought my performance was quite good."

"Because you'll work harder for a better grade next time," she said.

He glanced over at the bedside clock. "It's nearly lunchtime."

"Maybe we should do something," Lily said, stretching her arms over her head. "We could go into town."

"Or we could lie around by the pool," he suggested.

"Or we could have lunch in bed," she said.

"You think you might be taking this research thing a little too seriously?" he teased. "We can't spend all our time in bed."

Lily rolled over on her stomach and threw her arm over his chest, resting her chin on his shoulder. "You can never take science too seriously. What if Sir Isaac Newton's girlfriend told him he ought to go to lunch instead of sitting under that tree studying gravity? I have a responsibility to the world."

Aidan pulled her closer and nuzzled his nose into her fragrant hair. He'd only known Lily for a little more than a day, but he knew what he liked about her. She didn't take herself too seriously. Her revelation about Miranda Sinclair could have been enough to sour their relationship, but instead, it had only made her more attractive to him.

She wasn't afraid to admit she had flaws and even pointed them out with great honesty. But in his mind, nothing about her was flawed. She was perfect in her imperfections. Lily was a real woman, with a real heart and soul.

Aidan closed his eyes. He didn't know where the hell this was all leading. But he was willing to give it time—and the attention it needed. "We'll just lie here for a little while longer. Then we can decide what to do," he said.

He heard the familiar buzz of his cell phone and reached out to grab it from the bedside table. Lily had warned him that Miranda might try to call and as he scrolled through the missed calls, he recognized her number on five of them.

But this call was from his agent. He sat up. "I should really take this," he said. "I'm going to get some water. Do you want some?"

Lily nodded, then snuggled into the down pillows and closed her eyes. Aidan walked back to the small galley kitchen, then flipped open his phone. "Hi, Sam. What's up?"

"Where have you been? And why haven't you been answering your phone?"

"Sorry, I had it turned off."

"For two days?"

"I've just been busy. I'm on vacation."

"Well, I'm never on vacation when it comes to your career and you shouldn't be, either."

Though he loved having an agent like Sam, always on the job, never one to pass an opportunity by, there were times when Aidan just needed to decompress. "What's up? What did you want?"

"Well, first of all, let me preface this by saying I rarely get involved in a client's personal affairs. But I just had the strangest phone call from Miranda Sinclair. She claims that you and her goddaughter are getting married."

"Married?" Aidan laughed out loud. "Where would she get an idea like that?"

"From her goddaughter. Your fiancée! She was like a crazy woman on the phone. She said she's been trying to call you and she wanted to know if I knew how to get in touch with you. I thought you were going to talk to her about a new project."

Was this what Lily had meant by payback? "Don't worry. I'll straighten this out."

"Well, you'd better do it quick. The story is already out there. I've had two calls to confirm it from *US Weekly.* What do you want me to tell them?"

"Tell them it's not true," Aidan said. "I'm not getting married. You can quote me on that."

"All right. I got you a meeting with the guys over at Altamont Pictures. They have an interesting new project that I think you might be good for. It's not an action flick. I set it up for tomorrow."

"I can't take a meeting tomorrow," Aidan said.

"Why not?"

"Because I'm in New York. On vacation."

"Fly back."

"No," Aidan said. "I want to stay here. Tell them we'll have to reschedule."

"This is a great opportunity, Aidan. You told me you wanted something different and I got it for you. If this is about some woman, then I—"

"If they really want me, they'll wait. I have to go. I'll call you later in the week. Bye, Sam."

Aidan turned off the phone and opened the refrigerator, grabbing two bottles of designer water. He knew Lily was simply trying to get Miranda all riled up, but

Aidan wondered why the mention of engagement and marriage didn't seem to bother him at all. He hadn't known Lily for long, but the one thing he did know was that she was even less interested in marriage than he was.

At the last minute, Aidan put his phone inside the fridge and shut the door. When he got back to the bed, he sat down in the center and pressed the cold bottle against Lily's bare arm.

"You'll be happy to know that the press will be announcing our engagement soon."

She opened her eyes, then pushed up on her elbows. "What did you say?"

"There's a rumor flying around Hollywood that we're going to get married."

Lily sat up and grabbed the blanket bunched at the end of the bed, pulling it up around her naked body. "Oh, no."

"Oh, yes. Do you know anything about that?"

"That's not the way this was supposed to work," Lily explained, the color high in her cheeks. "She wasn't supposed to tell anyone. I just said that to get back at her for meddling."

"What did you say, Lily?" Aidan asked, handing her the bottle of water.

A blush slowly rose in her cheeks. "I called Miranda and told her we were running away and getting married. And then, I told you and Luisa not to answer the phone so she could stew about it for a while. I was going to call her back and tell her I was joking, but then we came out here and got…busy. I forgot."

"She's called me five times and now she's called my agent. And she must have called someone else, because it's leaked out to the press."

Lily pressed her palm to her forehead. "I'm sorry. I'm sorry, I really wasn't serious. It was the only thing I could think of that might make her crazy. You don't know what it's like with her. I call her my scary godmother."

Aidan shook his head. "There's only one thing to do."

"I'll call her," Lily said. "I'll explain everything."

"No, I think we should just get married," Aidan said, trying to maintain a serious expression. "It's easier than trying to explain everything. And the press will never believe us anyway. Yeah, I think that's just the thing to do."

She stared at him, her mouth agape, her eyes wide. Aidan reached out and hooked his finger beneath her chin, then closed her mouth. A smile slowly curled her lips. "It would make her really mad," she said. "She's been planning my wedding since the day I graduated from college. She doesn't have any children of her own and she's just dying to start making up the invitation list."

"It sounds like she loves you very much," Aidan said.

Lily wrapped her arms around her legs and rested her chin on her knees. "She does. I know that. And I know she only wants me to be happy. I should be grateful. But sometimes she just gets on my last nerve."

"Are you happy now?" Aidan asked.

Lily glanced over at him and nodded. "I am."

"Good," he said. "Is there anything I can do to make you happier?"

Lily paused before she answered. "You could drive me into town and buy me a toasted coconut gelato. There's a shop in Eastport that sells the best gelato."

"You're pretty easy to please," he said.

It wouldn't be difficult to fall in love with Lily, Aidan mused. With her, everything was easy. He didn't care that his name and hers would be all over the press in a few days. And he didn't care that her godmother seemed to be intent on sizing him up as a husband for Lily. Hell, hanging around Lily, sharing a bed with her, was worth a little hassle.

He leveled a serious gaze at her. "So are we having a big wedding or a small ceremony with just friends and family?"

"Actually, we're running away to get married," Lily said. "I didn't say where. We'll have to figure that out. Maybe Canada?"

"A Canadian wedding. That sounds nice. I like Toronto. They have a great film festival up there. And a really big lake."

Lily giggled, wrapping her arms around his neck and pulling him back down on the bed. She softly bit his lower lip. "I think this is going to have to be one of those Hollywood engagements. We'll give it another hour and then we'll have to break it off. We'll just say we grew apart and we're still friends."

"Friends with benefits," he teased. "Really good benefits."

THE LITTLE village of Eastport was one of Lily's favorite spots in the whole world. It was known for its quaint antique shops, and Lily used to spend Saturdays during her teenage summers searching for treasures in the dusty corners and deep shelves. She'd ride her bike into town, along the windswept roads, eat lunch at the luncheonette and ride back home before dinner.

Some of the shopkeepers she'd known back then were gone, but there were still many familiar faces she stopped to see whenever she was in town.

"I never understood the whole thing with antiques," Aidan said, staring down at a display of silver spoons. "Why buy something old when you can have something new?"

"It's the history," Lily said. She pointed to a silver teapot in a case behind the counter and the clerk brought it out. "Hold this."

Aidan did as he was told, sending Lily a perplexed frown. "If I rub it will a genie come out?"

"Think about the person who first owned this," she said. "It's dated from the 1780s. A man made this with his own hands. And the person who owned it probably lived through the Revolutionary War. Maybe she brought this with her as a bride when she came from England. She might have had a son who fought in the war or maybe her husband did. She was alive when this country was born. She warmed her hands with that pot on a cold winter night. No one will ever know her name or what she experienced in life, but she had a life once and this teapot was part of that life."

He stared at the teapot for a long time, then nodded. "I see what you mean." He looked up at the clerk. "How much is it?"

"Thirty-five hundred," the clerk said.

"I'll take it," Aidan replied.

Lily gasped. "What are you doing?"

"I want the pot," he said.

"Why? You don't collect antiques."

He pulled out his wallet and laid a credit card on the counter. "I just want it. I want something to remember this day by. And I liked the story."

The woman packed it up in a small box, then gave him the receipt to sign. When they walked out of the shop into the sunshine, Lily turned to him. "You're crazy," she said. "You probably could have gotten a better price if you had bargained with her."

"Maybe," he replied. "I'm the crazy owner of an antique teapot." He drew a deep breath. "You know what I'd really like to find? My grandfather used to have this bank. It was a soldier and you put your coin on his gun and then hit a lever and the coin would fly into a hole in a tree and drop down into the trunk."

"There's a shop just down the street that specializes in toys," she said. "Mechanical banks are very collectible."

"I used to play with that bank for hours. I was in college when he died and I asked my mother if I could have it, but they'd already donated a lot of his things to charity." He grabbed her hand and they strolled down the street, his teapot tucked beneath his arm. "This is fun. I usually don't like shopping, but with you, it's nice."

Lily linked her arm in his. "I hate shopping. But this isn't really shopping. It's more like treasure-hunting. You never know what you're going to find."

Though the morning had begun a bit strangely, Lily had managed to salvage the remainder of the day. She'd called Miranda and apologized for the silly trick she'd played and to her surprise her godmother was properly contrite, admitting that she might have gone a bit too far in her matchmaking. If Miranda expected an explanation of what was going on between Lily and Aidan, Lily refused to provide it. She simply told her godmother Aidan was a nice guy and they were having a good time.

Lily smiled to herself. She could imagine Miranda, back in California, left to speculate about the end results of her matchmaking. No doubt she'd grill Luisa about the sleeping arrangements, but Lily didn't really care. Maybe she ought to be grateful for the opportunity. It probably wouldn't have happened had Lily left it to destiny.

"Should we have dinner in town?" Aidan asked. "We passed an Italian restaurant when we drove in. I could go for pizza."

"That sounds good," Lily said. "We could get it to go and take it back to the house."

"That sounds even better," he said, wrapping his arm around her shoulder and pulling her close. He kissed the top of her head and for a fleeting moment, Lily felt as though her life was perfect. This was what it was supposed to feel like when a person was in love, this absolute contentment.

"That's a nice store," Lily said, pointing to an antique shop across the street. "They have a lot of old toys, too. Maybe we could find your bank. Or maybe—"

"Aidan?"

Aidan stopped and slowly turned at the sound of the woman's voice. A leggy blonde stood in the doorway of the shop they'd just passed. She pulled off her sunglasses and hurried toward them.

"I thought that was you!"

He stepped forward as she approached. "Brooke. Hi."

She threw her arms around his neck and gave him a hug. "What are you doing here? I expected to see a few people I knew from L.A., but not you. I didn't think you were the Hamptons type."

"Just here for a visit." He turned to Lily. "Lily, this is Brooke Farris. Brooke, this is my friend Lily Hart. I'm staying at her place."

Brooke glanced at Lily, gave her a dismissive smile, then turned her attention back to Aidan. "Why don't we see each other anymore? I think about you all the time. We used to have so much fun together."

Lily turned to Aidan, waiting for his reply. Why wasn't he dating this woman? She was beautiful, tall and slender...willowy, Lily decided. No matter how hard she tried, she'd never be willowy. And Brooke had blond hair and blindingly white teeth. Her makeup was perfect and her clothes looked as though they came right out of a fashion magazine.

"You know how it is," Aidan said. "Same old story. Busy. I've been out of town."

"Well, you make sure you call me when you get back. Hey, there's a big party out at Jack Simons's house tomorrow night. I'm staying in his guesthouse for the week. He's directing my next movie. You'll love it. Everyone is going to be there. I'll put your name on the list." She reached into her handbag and pulled out an envelope. "Here, take this. There are directions inside." She glanced over at Lily again. "And bring your friend. She's welcome, too."

Aidan watched as she walked off. When she turned and gave him a wave, he returned the gesture. Lily carefully observed them both, trying to figure out just what they might have meant to each other. Had they dated? Probably. Slept together? Any normal man would have gone for it. Been in love? Aidan didn't seem to be that happy to see her.

"She's lovely," Lily murmured.

Her words seemed to startle him out of a silent contemplation. He shrugged, then turned back to her. "I guess. She's not as pretty as you."

Until this moment, Lily had believed every compliment he'd given her, accepting every charming smile. But somehow, she couldn't bring herself to believe him. "You don't have to say that. I know that I'm not as…gorgeous as she is."

"What the hell are you talking about?" Aidan replied. "You're every bit as beautiful. Even more so, because you're a nice person, too."

"Oh, yes," Lily said, forcing a laugh, "a nice personality always gets a girl more men than a beautiful face and body."

"Stop it," Aidan said in a cajoling tone.

"No, you stop it," Lily answered back, feeling her temper rise. At the very least, he should be honest with her. She deserved that much. "Don't you think it's just a little condescending to pretend that I'm in the same ballpark as she is?"

Lily swallowed a lump of emotion. It had been so easy to lose herself in the fantasy, but the truth of the matter was, Aidan could have his pick of women. She was just the one he was sleeping with at the moment, until someone better came along. She could handle that, as long as he was honest.

She'd promised herself she wouldn't let it matter, that when it all finally came to an end, she'd be satisfied and move on. But she didn't want to imagine him leaving her for another woman, someone more beautiful, more self-assured.

He grabbed her hand and pulled her along the sidewalk until he found a quiet spot out of the view of passing pedestrians. "Listen," he said, his tone calm and measured. "If I wanted to be with a woman like that, I would be. I want to be with you. I *am* with you. End of story. Now, can we get back to the fun we were having and forget about that woman?"

Lily stared up into his eyes, the truth written there plainly for her to see. Every instinct told her not to trust him. He would hurt her in the end, Lily knew it deep down in her soul. "I'm sorry," she finally said. "I'm tired. We haven't been sleeping much lately. And I got up really early this morning."

Aidan smoothed his palm over her cheek, then kissed her gently. "Maybe we should get that pizza and head home," he suggested.

Lily nodded. It was simpler to pretend everything would be all right when she was alone with Aidan. Out in the real world, Lily was forced to admit the chances of hanging on to a man like him were slim at best.

Sooner or later, he'd realize she was just an ordinary girl. The things he found so charming or captivating about her would fade and he'd be left to wonder why he was even attracted in the first place. This was a vacation romance and everyone knew what happened to those—they ended when the vacation was over.

6

"Miss Lily? Miss Lily?"

Lily rolled over, pulling the blanket up around her nose and moaning softly. She slowly drifted back to sleep, but an incessant knocking nagged at her. Opening one eye, she noticed the sun streaming through the doors of the pool house.

"Miss Lily?"

Pushing up on her elbow, she glanced over to the other side of the bed. Aidan was already up and gone. "I'm up," she called out to Luisa. "Come on in."

Luisa hurried inside, the cordless phone clutched in her hand. "I'm sorry to disturb you, but it's Miss Miranda. She said it was an emergency."

Lily looked over at the clock. It was only 7:00 a.m. out in L.A., too early for Miranda to be out of bed. A sliver of fear shot through her. "What kind of emergency?" she asked, holding out her hand for the phone.

Luisa shook her head, a look of anxiety on her face. "She wouldn't say."

Lily put the phone up to her ear. "Miranda? What's wrong? Are you all right? Where are you?"

"Did you see it this morning? Rachel just called and she said the booksellers on the east coast are going crazy trying to order more of your book."

"What?" Lily rubbed the sleep out of her eyes. "Miranda, what is the emergency?"

"Your book!" Miranda cried. "They were talking about it on *Talk to Me* this morning. You know, that talk show I hate with those whiney women. Well, they were discussing your book. And now, booksellers are getting orders they can't fill, and they're going after their distributors and it's just crazy. Rachel—she handles publicity for the publisher—she called this morning and said they want to capitalize on this. They need you to go on *Talk to Me*."

Lily ran her hands through her hair as she tried to understand everything Miranda was saying. "I—I can't be on television," she said. "I mean, maybe I could do a book-signing, but that's it. As soon as they see me, they'll never believe I wrote that book."

"But you did write the book," Miranda said.

"I know, I know. But isn't it better just to keep my identity a secret? I didn't want to write a sex book, Miranda. That was your idea."

"Lily, if you promote this book, they'll want to buy another book from you, and then another. They like to employ authors who help sell their own books. Why do you think I'm on the road six months out of the year?"

"You really think I should do this?" she asked.

"Yes, you should. Rachel is going to call you later today. She'll take the train out to see you and you'll set up a plan. They want you on *Talk to Me* early next week. Get yourself something nice to wear. I'm going to make an appointment for you at my salon in Southampton. They'll do your hair and give you a facial and manicure."

"Yeah, and I'll just pick up a brand-new personality while I'm at it."

"Ask Aidan for help," Miranda suggested. "He's managed to get some amazing performances out of third-rate actresses. Maybe he can help you. That is, if he's still there with you?"

"Yes, Miranda, he's still here."

"Is he with you right now?" she asked. "Never mind, I'll just ask Luisa what's going on. She's much more forthcoming with details. She said you sleep in the pool house with him. Darling, you can sleep in the house. I don't mind and I—"

"Goodbye, Miranda."

"Call me later and tell me what Rachel said. I want to know exactly what they have planned for you. Don't let them overschedule you and don't even consider the second- and third-tier talk shows. And whatever you do, don't wear white, it will make you look like a whale."

"Miranda, I know what to do. I've been coordinating your publicity with Rachel for years now."

"Yes," she said. "Just don't do anything I wouldn't do."

Lily hung up the phone and tossed it on the bed, then flopped back into the pillows. She covered her face with her hands. What was she going to do? It was one thing to write the book, but it was another to defend it.

Yes, she believed in everything she'd written. Women should have the power to get what they wanted from men sexually, the same way men had done for years.

But she hadn't lived the book…except that day on the plane with Aidan. And she was almost certain that particular piece of research could never be replicated with another man. They had both been in the right place at the right time.

Her mind wandered back to the previous afternoon, to their encounter with Aidan's ex-lover. "Brooke Farris would know what to do," she muttered. With her long blond hair and her perfect white teeth and her perky boobs. Brooke Farris probably loved going on talk shows as much as she loved sleeping with Aidan. "Maybe I should just hire Brooke Farris to play Lacey St. Claire. That would solve all my problems."

"Is everything all right?"

Startled, Lily glanced over to see Aidan, outlined by the sunshine. He walked to the bed and stood over her, dressed in shorts and running shoes, drinking a glass of orange juice. His body gleamed with a sheen of sweat. "No," she said, wondering how much he'd heard.

"Luisa said Miranda called with an emergency. Do you have to fly back?"

Lily shook her head. "No, everything is fine with her. Not so fine with me."

He sat down on the edge of the mattress, bracing his hand on the other side of her body and leaning in to kiss her. His lips were sweet with juice. "What's wrong?"

"*The Ten-Minute Seduction* was discussed on a very

popular talk show this morning and the booksellers have been clamoring to order more copies. My publisher wants me to do a publicity tour."

"That's great," he said. "Isn't it?"

"Do I look like the kind of woman who could have written that book?"

His gaze lazily drifted from her face down to her bare breasts and back up again. "You look exactly like that kind of woman. You *are* that kind of woman."

"I was tricked into researching and writing the book. And now, I'm getting tricked into promoting it."

"Lily, you don't have to do anything you don't want to do. I'll back you on that. If you don't want to promote the book, don't promote it. Just say no."

She drew a deep breath, then sighed. "I've never had a source of income outside of what Miranda pays me. And I've wanted to get my own place for a few years now. I've saved some money, but if the book does well, then maybe I'll have enough to buy a little house. I'd have a life of my own." Lily reached up and smoothed her palm over his cheek. "Will you help me? Miranda said you could make even the worst actresses look good. Do you think you could turn me into Lacey St. Claire?"

"Remind me to thank Miranda for the compliment," Aidan said, setting the empty glass on the bedside table.

"That's all it really is, right? Just acting. If I'm not that woman, than I can pretend to be her. You're the director. Direct me."

"You're kidding, right?"

"I'm dead serious. They want me to go on the show

next week. I have to be ready. I have to look like a...a seductress."

Aidan regarded her with a dubious look. Then he grudgingly nodded. "All right. I have to take a shower first but—" He paused, then grinned. "Or we could take a shower together. Have you ever made love in a shower?"

"No," Lily said, feeling a warm blush rising in her cheeks.

"The shower is big enough for two," Aidan said. "We could call this lesson one. Come on, Lacey. Lure me into the shower and have your way with me."

Lily threw the covers off and scrambled to her feet. "All right. This is a start. Take your clothes off."

Aidan slowly shook his head. "You take my clothes off. You're the one in training here." He stood back, his arms crossed over his chest, his gaze raking her body. "God, you are beautiful in the morning," he murmured.

With Aidan, it was easy, she mused. He made it obvious that he wanted her as much as she wanted him. When it came to sex, she didn't have to think. She just felt. Lily pushed up on her toes and kissed him, her palm sliding down his belly to his crotch. She rubbed suggestively, until he began to get hard beneath the silky fabric of his basketball shorts. "I'm taking a shower," she said in her most seductive tone. "You can stay out here or you can join me."

"That's all right," he replied. "I don't need a shower."

Lily raised her eyebrow. "Oh, but you do. You need me to run my soapy hands all over your naked body and get you nice and clean so that we can—"

Aidan grabbed her and kissed her, stopping her come-on with his lips and his tongue. When he finally drew away, Lily ran toward the bathroom. He took up the chase and she screamed when he caught her around the waist and carried her the rest of the way.

When the water had warmed, Aidan kicked off his shoes and stripped out of his shorts, then drew her into the glass-block shower. His mouth found hers again and he kissed her, hungry with desire. Lily arched against him as his lips trailed over her shoulder and onto her breasts.

But when he moved lower, Lily grabbed his hair and forced him to straighten. "I'm supposed to seduce you," she said. "Give me a chance."

She slowly stroked him as she explored his body with her lips and tongue. The water made him slick and before long, he was fully aroused and moaning with desire. Lily knew exactly what would drive him wild and when she closed her lips over the head of his shaft, he gasped, his hands braced on the wall of the shower, his eyes closed.

If this was the last man she'd know intimately, Lily could live with that. The memories of what they shared were so deeply etched into her mind she knew she'd be able to recall every caress, every reaction, just by closing her eyes.

She tempted him with her lips and her tongue, surprised by how easily she could bring him to the edge. And then, she took him too close. Aidan grabbed her arms and pulled her to her feet, his eyes closed, his jaw tense. Lily watched as he struggled to maintain control.

He opened his eyes and smiled, his gaze clouded with desire. "Stay right there," he murmured.

When he returned to the shower, he had a condom. He tore the package open and quickly sheathed himself. Then he gently drew her against him, his fingers slipping between her legs.

Every nerve in her body tingled, his touch causing her pulse to race. He could read her reactions and when she had reached the point of no return, he picked her up and wrapped her legs around his waist.

Slowly, Aidan entered her. The feel of him deep inside her was like nothing she'd ever experienced before. It was absolute surrender. The fears and insecurities that had kept her from loving him were gone. Why couldn't she feel this way all the time, as if there were no way anything could come between them?

The sensations coursing through her obliterated rational thought, and, a moment later, she was caught in the vortex of her release. Lily's body went boneless and it was all she could do to hold on to Aidan, the water making her hands and arms slick. A moment later, he found his own release, pressing her back against the wall of the shower as he drove into her one last time.

They clung to each other beneath the shower, both of them trembling in the aftermath of their orgasms. Lily felt tears fill her eyes and she let herself cry, knowing they would be hidden by the water.

She didn't want to believe she'd never experience this kind of passion with another man. This was the man she wanted in her life, yet she knew the odds were firmly against them. Her parents had loved each other once, they'd probably felt this kind of passion in each other's arms, but it hadn't lasted.

A fantasy could take her just so far. How long could she live inside it before the real world intruded? Lily knew there probably wouldn't be a happy ending to this affair. But it was wonderful while it lasted, wasn't it?

AIDAN stared up at the ceiling of the pool house, watching the blades of the fan as they spun into a blur. Lily had been closed inside Miranda's office with the publicist for the past two hours and he'd found himself restless and uneasy.

Since they'd returned from town the previous afternoon, he'd noticed a subtle shift in their relationship. He couldn't put his finger on it, but there was a look in her eyes when she met his gaze. What was it? Not sadness. Resignation, maybe?

Though they'd made love in the shower that morning, he sensed desperation in her desire, as if she wanted to prove something to herself—and maybe to him. Aidan rewound their encounter with Brooke.

He hadn't been happy to see her. He'd been polite and unresponsive to her obvious overtures. Though he and Brooke had dated for a month or two last year, and shared the same bed on a number of occasions, he'd never really considered her a serious relationship.

Hell, he'd never had a serious relationship. He'd had dating relationships, he'd had sexual relationships, but none of them had ventured into the realm of *serious*.

Aidan drew a ragged breath and covered his eyes with his arm. This felt serious, though.

When he was with Lily, he didn't want to be anywhere else. In truth, he was almost afraid to leave her, afraid that what they had found together might suddenly evaporate. They'd spent three nights and two days together. At this point in every other relationship, he was usually looking for a way out. But with Lily, he was still trying to figure a way in.

Aidan rolled off the bed and walked to the kitchen. A search through the beverages in the pool house fridge produced a bottle of imported beer. He had to give Miranda credit. She knew how to keep a pool house stocked for male guests. As he walked past the bed, he grabbed the script he'd brought along from L.A.

He tried to concentrate on the script, reading the same page again and again. But his thoughts were focused on Lily. Aidan wanted to check up on her, but it felt wrong to disturb her. He was still a houseguest, nothing more. Maybe as her boyfriend, he might have had the right. But he had no official status in her life.

Still, he was at least her friend. And as a friend, he knew how relentless the publicity machine could be, the interviews, the appearances. He could offer her some advice and guidance. Over the years, he'd had to do his fair share to promote a movie, although not nearly as much as the lead actors and actresses did. But it was the part of his job that he hated, the commercial part. He'd become a director because he wanted to see his vision on film and wanted others to experience it, as well.

Publicity always seemed to be a scam, an attempt to lure people into the theater under false pretenses. The promos for his films never really portrayed his work in a true light. And the actors always spoke in such glowing terms that it wasn't a surprise some audience members walked away disappointed. There was something to be said for seeing a movie with a completely open mind.

It was like the way he'd walked into this relationship with Lily: neither one of them had had any expectations, beyond a few hours of fun at twenty thousand feet. And when there was a promise of more, he accepted their relationship for what it was—for as long as it lasted.

Was that why he was so confused? Without a point of reference, he had no way of judging what they shared together. Was this love? Friendship? Or just overwhelming desire? Suddenly, it was important to put a name to it.

He strolled out to the pool to find Lily standing near the edge, staring into the water. She seemed lost in her own thoughts and didn't notice his approach.

"Hey, there. Are you done?"

Startled, Lily looked up, then shook her head. "No. We've got a bunch of stuff to go over yet. She's just calling her office to check her messages."

"How is it going?"

"Considering that I hate to fly, I'm not making things very easy for her. I'm thinking they should get me one of those big tour buses or maybe a Winnebago."

"When do you think you'll finish?"

She shrugged. "I don't know. I'm sorry. I didn't think it would take this long. We haven't had dinner yet. Luisa left some things in the fridge. Or you could run into town and get something."

"No problem," Aidan said. "I can wait. And I don't need you to entertain me." He reached out and slipped his arm around her waist. "Although, I enjoy it when you do."

"Why don't you go to that party?" she said, evading his touch. "There will be people there you know. Have some fun. And I'll be here when you get back."

He reached out for her again, only this time, he pulled her against him. "Those parties are never fun, Lily. And there's no one there I want to see. Everything I want is right here."

"But isn't it good to network?"

She seemed determined to get rid of him. Considering he didn't have another film lined up, maybe it wouldn't be a bad idea to stop by. Hell, he wasn't at the point in his career where he could refuse an invitation to a Jack Simons party. When he was with Lily, it was easy to forget he had a career.

"I'll go if you come with me," he said.

"I can't."

"We'll go together, after you're finished. Hey, going to a party like this would be good training. If you can make conversation with a group of self-absorbed Hollywood types, than you can talk to anyone. And they always have really good food."

To his surprise, Lily considered his suggestion for a long moment, then nodded. "All right. Why don't you go on ahead and I'll join you when I'm done? You can take the Jeep."

"How are you going to get there?"

"Luisa is still here. I'll get a ride with her."

He reached out and rubbed her forearms, staring down into her eyes. Why was she doing this? It was almost as if she was deliberately pushing him away, sending him back to the world he'd left behind in L.A. Was this a test, to see if he wanted to spend the evening with Brooke instead of her? Or was she simply giving him something to do with his time?

"You promise you'll come?"

"I promise," she said.

He studied her face, searching for any clue to her feelings. "I don't want her," he murmured. "I just want to make that clear, if that's what this is all about."

"I know," Lily said.

Her reply told the whole story. She'd obviously been thinking about Brooke. "What is this about?" She glanced away, but Aidan gently turned her gaze back to his. "Talk to me, Lily. I know something is bothering you. You can be honest with me."

She turned and walked along the edge of the pool, staring back down into the water as if the answers were all there. "I like you," she finally said, refusing to look at him as she spoke. "And that's a dangerous thing because it makes me want to spend more time with you. But the more time I spend with you, the more I like you."

"That's usually the way it is," Aidan said. "What's wrong with that?"

"When we finally go our separate ways, I'm going to miss you."

Aidan slowly walked to her, then took her hand in his. "And what do you want to do about that, Lily? Maybe we should make a plan."

"Or maybe we should just let it go," she suggested, the words rushing out of her. "We know how it will end. You'll be on location and I'll be in L.A. and we'll realize that it's not as good as it used to be. It will never be as good as this week in the Hamptons."

Aidan knew she was probably right. But he wanted to believe that someday, someone would come along and change that. He wanted to believe Lily might just be the one. But if she didn't believe it, then how could he?

"I think I will go to that party," he murmured.

If Lily was so determined to construct a wall between them, why was he so intent on breaking it down? Hell, he didn't need complications in his life. It would be so much easier just to accept their relationship as something with a beginning and an end.

"Good," she said.

"You know how to get there?"

"I went to a charity event there a few summers back. I know where it is. Luisa will drop me off on her way home."

Not that it made any difference. He didn't expect Lily to show, anyway. He'd get home later tonight and she'd come up with some excuse for bailing. And then, she'd find a reason to sleep in her own bed that night. And by tomorrow morning, he'd be making plans to leave. He could feel it going bad and yet there was nothing he could do to stop it.

"I'd better get back," she said. She ran her fingers through her hair and pasted a smile on her face. "I'll see you later."

Aidan was already tired of talking around what was obviously a problem. He grabbed her hand and pulled her into his arms, then kissed her, making sure she knew exactly how he felt. His hands grasped her face and he molded her mouth to his, his tongue delving deep.

This was how it was supposed to be between them, the attraction running so deep that neither one of them could deny it. Maybe he just needed to keep reminding her how good it was. "Whatever you do, you remember that," he murmured. "Remember how that feels."

He let go of Lily and she stumbled back, her eyes wide, her breath coming in tiny gasps. Aidan turned and walked back toward the pool house. It was her move now. If she didn't make one, at least he knew where he stood. If she did, then they'd still have a chance.

LILY HAD been to Jack Simons's house on one other occasion and she'd spent the night sitting in a quiet corner of the terrace, watching as Miranda flitted between celebrities and socialites. Though Miranda had always tried to draw her into conversation, Lily never felt she had anything important to say, so she preferred to watch.

It was so much easier to be herself when she didn't have to struggle to act interesting. Maybe it was all left over from a childhood spent sitting on the sidelines, watching an odd array of characters come in and out of her life. At least it had given her plenty of material for her novel. Maybe she'd find more inspiration at this party.

"How do I look?" she asked, turning to Luisa.

"You look lovely," the housekeeper said.

"You're not just saying that, are you?"

She shook her head. "I have always thought that you were a beautiful girl, Lily. And I wondered if you'd ever realize that yourself." She paused. "It's difficult, I know. Miranda loves to have the spotlight on her. Sometimes, there's not much light left over for those around her."

Lily smoothed her hands over the front of the dress she wore. She'd gone into Miranda's closet, looking for something casual yet expensive, something that would make her look as if she belonged. She'd found a lovely sleeveless raw-silk dress in a deep teal with a coppery sheen and she accented it with a chunky necklace and matching earrings that she knew had cost Miranda a bundle at Bloomingdale's. The only things that came from her own wardrobe were the sandals.

Lily swallowed hard. What had ever possessed her to go to this party? It had seemed like such a brave idea at home. She deserved to be there. Aidan wanted her there. And she wanted to show Brooke Farris that Aidan had chosen her. It wasn't as if she were crashing the party. Jack Simons was a friend of Miranda's.

She needed to do this for herself—and for Lacey St. Claire. Over the next few months, she'd be socializing with complete strangers. If she couldn't manage outside her cozy little comfort zone, then she'd have no chance of making her book tour a success.

Lily tried to summon her confidence, but all she was left with was a sick feeling in her stomach. "You know, he's probably already on his way home," she said. "I should go back. Take me back home, Luisa."

"Well, we might as well see if he's still there. I'll wait outside for ten minutes and if you don't come out, I'll know you've found him."

Drawing a nervous breath, Lily nodded. If she felt uneasy, she'd walk inside, use the bathroom and walk right back out again. She held her breath as Luisa turned into the driveway, her hands clutching at the designer bag she'd borrowed from Miranda.

Parties in the Hamptons were always huge and expensive affairs. The bigger the house, the more over-the-top the party. Spotlights illuminated the facade of the stone mansion and huge floral arrangements flanked the wide front doors. Somewhere in the distance, a band played, the sound of the saxophone drifting on the night breeze.

When she got to the door, a security guard stopped her. "Do you have your invitation?"

"I'm meeting Aidan Pierce," she said.

He checked the list. "I have Aidan Pierce, but no guest with him. Sorry."

Lily frowned. Brooke must have neglected to add her to the list as she'd promised. Now that Lily was here, she didn't feel like leaving. "Miranda Sinclair," she said, taking on an irritated tone and tipping her chin up. It was worth a try. Miranda was usually invited to all the big summer parties.

"Here you are," he said, nodding. "Enjoy the party, Miss Sinclair."

The house didn't really qualify as a house. It wasn't even a mansion. She had just entered a modern-day castle. The home served only one purpose—to prove to the world how wealthy and powerful its owner was. There were fresh flowers everywhere and greenery strung from the two-story staircase.

A waiter appeared at her side and offered her a glass of champagne. Lily gulped it down and then took another. Everywhere she looked, she saw familiar faces—movie stars, musicians and celebrities who mixed easily with the new-money socialites from the city.

As she passed one of the many buffet tables, Lily picked up a canapé and popped it into her mouth. Then she found a spot near the fireplace and sipped her champagne as she searched the room for Aidan.

"My stylist was talking about it. She told me I had to read it, so I picked up a copy when I went into the city yesterday. I can't tell you how liberating it was."

Lily didn't mean to eavesdrop, but the three ladies standing next to her were talking so loudly it was impossible not to.

"But does it work?"

"I seduced my husband last night in less than ten minutes. He's always so tired that getting him even to consider sex is a major event. But he was definitely interested. For the whole night. And the next morning, too. It was the best sex we've had in years."

Lily stepped closer to the group. "Excuse me, I didn't mean to overhear, but are you talking about *The Ten-Minute Seduction*?"

"We are," the brunette said. "Have you read it?"

"I—I have," Lily said. "Actually, I wrote it."

"You're Lacey St. Claire?"

Lily nodded. "That's a pen name. Lily Hart. That's my real name."

"Oh my God, I loved the book. It was so informative, so straightforward. I always felt uneasy about initiating sex, but this really released me from my inhibitions. I honestly do believe that men like women who take control. I can't tell you how this has changed my marriage."

"That's wonderful," Lily said.

"I'm Cynthia Woodridge and these are my friends Camille Rayburn and Whitney DeVoe."

Lily shook their hands, stunned that she'd actually met someone who had bought and read her book. And a little flattered that they were interested in what she had to say. It was an odd feeling, though not unwelcome. "It's a pleasure," she said.

"You have to come to my book club," Cynthia begged. "I've been talking about this book nonstop since I read it yesterday. I've ordered copies for all my friends—married and divorced. You're here in the Hamptons for the summer? How perfect could this be?"

Lily nodded. "I'm staying with Miranda Sinclair."

"How lovely," Cynthia said, uninterested in talking about Miranda. "Now, tell me. How many men have you seduced using your techniques?"

Lily laughed. "I never kiss and tell," she said. "Let's just say, I use my powers prudently."

"Is there anyone here you want to seduce?" Camille asked. "I'd love to see how you do it."

Lily was taken aback by the request. But then, maybe there was a way to make this work to her advantage. "I suppose I could look around and see if there's anyone I'm interested in." She carefully scanned the party guests, looking for Aidan and desperately hoping he was still at the party.

She grabbed another glass of champagne from a waiter, then turned and smiled at the ladies. "I'm going to look outside," she said.

The trio followed her at a discreet distance, through the huge living room and out onto the terrace. She finally spotted Aidan sitting on the low wall that surrounded the terrace. Brooke was standing next to him, clothed in a clingy slip dress with a neckline cut nearly to her navel.

The three women came up behind her. "There," Lily said. "I like that one."

"I don't know him," Cynthia said. "But he's gorgeous. Do you know him, girls?"

Her friends shook their heads. "That's Brooke Farris with him, though," Whitney said. "God, I hate her. Look at the dress she's wearing. Could she make herself any more obvious? Everyone knows she isn't wearing anything underneath."

"Go ahead," Camille said. "Steal him away from her. I'd love to see it."

Lily knew how fast the Hamptons' grapevine worked. If she managed to pull this off convincingly, every woman at the party would have heard about it before they left for the evening. And by tomorrow afternoon, Lacey St. Claire would have the reputation she so desperately needed.

"What are you going to do first?" Camille asked.

"Catch his eye," Lily said.

"That's right," Cynthia said. "Eye contact is very important."

Lily stared across the terrace at Aidan. Brooke was speaking to him, but he didn't seem to be paying attention to her. Every now and then, he'd glance at the crowd. Was he looking for her?

She waited, stepping a bit closer. Suddenly, their eyes met and their gazes held. "There," Lily murmured, a smile playing at her lips.

"Look," Camille said. "It worked."

He slowly stepped away from Brooke and walked toward her. Lily heard Brooke call his name, but she kept her attention fixed on Aidan. They met in the middle of the terrace. She reached up and placed her hand on his chest. "Hello," she murmured. "I don't think we've met."

"We haven't?"

"I'm Lacey St. Claire," she said.

"Aidan Pierce." He leaned closer to whisper in her ear. "I wasn't sure you'd come."

"Take my hand," Lily said.

"All right." Aidan did as he was told, lacing his fingers

through hers and drawing them up to his mouth. "There's music. Would you like to dance, Miss St. Claire?"

Lily nodded. "I'd love to dance."

He grabbed her champagne glass and set it on a nearby table, then tucked her hand into the crook of his arm before leading her to the dance floor.

She'd never danced with a man before. There had been boys at high school dances, but this was different. When he held her, it was with a strength she'd never felt, as if her body belonged to him. He gently moved her across the floor, her hand tucked into his, his fingers splayed across the small of her back.

"I'm glad you came," he said. "I didn't think you would."

"I'm glad I came, too," she said. "I like dancing with you."

"I'm not very good," he said.

"You're wonderful." She nuzzled her face into his shoulder.

"You look beautiful in that dress," he said. "When I saw you standing there, I couldn't believe my eyes." His hand slid lower, to rest on her backside.

Lily looked up into his eyes and smiled. He always knew exactly what to say to make her feel comfortable. Out of all the beautiful women at this party, he was dancing with her, he was holding her. He bent closer and kissed her, his tongue dampening her lips.

"I think I've had enough of this party," Aidan said. "Let's get out of here." He grabbed her hand and pulled her along through the crowd, down the steps of the terrace to the lawn. She glanced back at Cynthia, Camille and Whitney and they stared at her, openmouthed. Brooke was also watching them from the edge of the terrace, her gaze fixed on Lily in a murderous glare.

"Where are we going?" she asked.

"I don't know," Aidan said. "Someplace where we can be alone. Right now, I have to touch you and I can't do it in the middle of a crowd."

"We could just go home," she suggested.

"No, that would take too long."

The lawn was decorated with tents, straight out of the Arabian nights. Sheer fabric draped over the sides, billowing in the breeze and revealing the occupants inside. But Aidan walked past them all, headed toward a low glass building near the tennis courts.

When they got closer, Lily could see it was a greenhouse. Aidan opened the door and they stepped inside. The air was humid and the scent of flowers filled her head. "Are you sure we can come in here?"

"The door wasn't locked," he said. "I'd consider that an invitation to at least look around."

Lily could barely see him, the lights from the tennis courts blocked by lush greenery. He circled her waist with his hands and lifted her up to sit on the edge of a workbench.

"Do you know how much I missed you tonight?" His lips were hot on her skin, his tongue tracing a line from her mouth to the base of her neck.

"Tell me," she said, arching back.

"The whole time I was here, I wanted to be somewhere else." His fingers tore at the shoulder of her dress, pulling it down until her breast was exposed.

"I missed you, too," she said, running her fingers though his hair. "I'm used to having you around."

He grabbed her face and kissed her hungrily. "What are we going to do about this?" he murmured, his lips against hers.

Until now, they'd avoided any discussion of the future. But it was becoming more and more apparent that they'd have to address it sooner or later. What would happen at the end of the week? Would they still feel this overwhelming desire or would the demands of real life make this impossible to sustain?

"Make love to me," Lily whispered.

"Here?"

"Here," she said. "I need to feel you inside me."

Though they risked being discovered, Aidan took his time, slowly seducing her with his fingers until Lily ached for release. And when he finally buried himself in her warmth, he held her close and whispered her name.

Though their lovemaking had been intense in the past, Aidan seemed almost desperate to make a more intimate connection, to drive deeper, to find someplace that he'd left untouched.

Lily felt a wave of emotion overcome her. This man had turned her life upside down in the course of a few days. He'd made her believe that complete and utter happiness was possible. How would she survive once this was all taken away?

She clung to him, letting the sensations that coursed through her body smother the thoughts in her head. The pleasure that was just out of reach grew closer and Lily gasped as he increased his pace. His fingers bit into her hips and he pressed his lips to the curve of her neck, moaning with each thrust.

They were lost in the passion, both of them caught up in a spiraling storm of desire. It was raw and primal and Lily gave up trying to fight the waves of pleasure that raced through her body. When her orgasm finally came, it was deep and powerful and Aidan followed her, their bodies arching against each other until there was nothing left to give.

Lily gasped for breath and tried to slow her pounding heart. He'd never possessed her in such a fierce and determined manner, as if he wanted to prove that what they shared was unbreakable. Lily didn't know what it all meant. Maybe she'd never know.

But for now, they belonged to each other, body and soul. They'd dropped the last pretense of a casual affair and claimed each other as their own. No matter what happened, a part of him would always belong to her.

7

"WHAT DO you think of this one?" Lily asked. She held the dress up in front of her and stared at her reflection in the full-length mirror. "It has to be a little sexy, but sophisticated."

Miranda had called her favorite shop in Southampton and had them send over a selection of dresses for Lily's television interview the following week. The dresses were scattered over her bed, a riot of color and pattern that Lily couldn't seem to sort through. There were things that Lily definitely liked, but she wasn't sure if Lacey St. Claire would wear them.

"I like that one," Aidan said. He was stretched out on the other side of her bed, his nose buried in the latest issue of *Sports Illustrated*. He wore his usual uniform of shorts and flip-flops. "The Mets are playing tonight. We should go into the city and see the game."

"How can you think about baseball when I'm in the middle of a crisis?" she asked.

He peeked over the top of the magazine and rolled his eyes. "This is a crisis? I'll alert the news media."

She gave him a grudging smile. "All right. It's not a

crisis. Just a problem I have to solve. I want you tell me what you think. You're a man. You know what looks sexy on a woman. Remember, I'm Lacey St. Claire."

He stared at the dress for a long moment. "I can't tell. You'll have to try it on."

With a dramatic sigh, Lily tossed the dress on her bed and began to strip out of her clothes. Oddly, Aidan didn't seem to be interested in his magazine any longer. He watched her as she undressed, his gaze skimming over her body.

"Wait," he said as she picked up the dress. "I like this look. But without the bra and panties. Try that."

"That would go over really well on national television," she said.

"It doesn't matter what you wear," Aidan said. "You look good in anything. And nothing."

Leave it to Aidan to diffuse her anxiety with a romantic compliment. Lily crawled onto the bed and straddled his hips, then grabbed the magazine and threw it on the floor. "Why are you so nice to me?"

"Because I like you," he said. "I like you a lot. You're my favorite girl." He reached out and ran his hands down her arms. "The truth is—" He paused as if searching for the words he wanted to say. "The truth is…well, I think we should talk about the truth."

"That sounds serious," she teased. "I thought we weren't doing serious."

"Maybe we should try," he said, meeting her gaze. "I talked to my agent this morning and I'm going to have to go back to L.A. day after tomorrow. And I was wondering... I was wondering what was going to happen with us. Because I'd really like to keep seeing you."

"You would?" Lily asked, unable to keep from smiling. "What does that mean?"

"I don't know. It means I want to see you. What do *you* think it means?"

"It could mean you want to stop by every now and then and talk. It might mean you want to take me out to dinner and a movie on a Friday night. It might just mean you want to make a booty call every few weeks."

"A booty call? I don't make booty calls."

"All men make booty calls. It's hardwired into your DNA."

Aidan reached up and cupped her cheek in his palm. "It means that I don't want any of this to end—the talking, the touching, the kissing, the sleeping together."

"I don't, either," Lily said. She took a deep breath. "But I live here in the summer. My work is here. And I have this publicity tour, which is going to go on for about six weeks. And you'll probably be on location for your next film. I'm not sure how this is going to work."

"We'll make it work," he said.

"Maybe we were just meant to have a vacation romance," she said.

"Don't say that." He sat up and grabbed her waist, rolling her over to lie beside him. Bracing his hands on either side of her shoulders, Aidan stretched out on top of her. "Lily, I can't make this work if you don't believe in it."

"I want to believe," Lily murmured. "But I saw how my parents struggled. It was a long, slow, painful process and I'm not sure I could go through that and come out whole on the other side."

"So, you just want to let this go?"

Lily shook her head. "No. I want to believe we could make it work. But we have to be realistic. And honest with each other. I'm willing to try, but if it starts to go bad, then you have to promise we'll end it. No anger, no regrets, no trying to fix something that can't be fixed. We'll wish each other well and say goodbye."

From his expression, he obviously didn't care for her suggestion. But it would be all she could manage to keep herself from getting hurt. Relationships weren't easy under normal circumstances. Throw in her family history and his career and the odds for success fell even further. She just wanted to be ready for the worst. Was that wrong?

"All right," he said. He bent close and kissed her, a simple, gentle, undemanding kiss that sent a shiver of desire through her body. Who was she fooling? No matter how it ended, she'd be devastated. It would take her a lifetime to forget him.

"Will you help me practice my interview questions?" she asked.

He nodded. "Do you have a list?"

"Yeah, but I practiced those already. I need some new questions. Some unexpected questions. Just ask me anything, the more provocative the better."

He rolled off her, stretching out at her side and

throwing his leg over her hip. "Why did you decide to write this book?"

"That one was on the list," she said.

"All right. How many men were seduced in the name of research for this book?"

"None," Lily said.

He scoffed, giving her a dubious look. "None?"

"Until I met you, I hadn't been with a man for more than a year. I was waiting for the right guy to come along."

"And has he?"

"Maybe," she said. "I don't know. We'll have to give it time." She paused. "What about you? How many women have you seduced in your life?" She didn't really want to know the answer, but she was curious. A man like Aidan must have had plenty of opportunities.

"I'm asking the questions here," he teased. "Favorite sexual fantasy?"

Lily's eyes went wide. "Do you really think they're going to ask that?"

"They could," Aidan said. "Better answer, just in case."

She considered her answer for a long time. "I don't know. I guess I'm living it right now." She shook her head. "That's not a very good answer. A big bubble bath, a bottle of champagne and my favorite guy in the tub with me."

"Cute," Aidan said. "There have been some reports that you're sleeping with the very talented and handsome director Aidan Pierce. What do you really think of his movies?"

"I've seen them all at least five or six times and I think they're fabulous," Lily replied.

Aidan laughed, obviously assuming she'd just told a bald-faced lie. But it was the truth. Lily wondered if now was the time to confess her secret yearlong crush. *He'd* been her favorite sexual fantasy for an entire year, from the moment she'd first seen him across the airport lounge. Maybe someday she'd tell him, Lily mused. But only when it wouldn't make any difference.

"We've heard rumors that he's really good in the sack. Would you care to confirm that story?"

"I will neither confirm nor deny," Lily said. "But I will say he's a very good kisser." She ran her finger over his lower lip. "Who taught you how to kiss?"

"I took a class," he said.

"I'm serious," Lily said. "Who was it?"

He frowned. "Alison Armstrong. She was thirteen and I was eleven, maybe twelve. She had kissed a lot of boys and for some unknown reason, she turned her attentions on me."

"Smart girl."

"No. I was a really skinny, geeky kid," he said. He pointed to his teeth. "I had braces and glasses and wore these bright blue sneakers that I thought were really cool because they looked like something the Power Rangers might wear."

"I don't believe you," Lily said.

"It's true. So one day, Alison comes up to me and tells me she wants to meet me underneath the bleachers at the soccer field. I showed up, figuring she was going to ask if I would do her math homework or if she could borrow my movie camera, but she pulled me under the bleachers and kissed the crap out of me."

"Slut!" Lily cried.

"Oh, yeah," Aidan said. "She stuck her tongue in my mouth and I didn't know what the hell I was doing. But I went with it. And pretty soon, I got the hang of it. And then we met for the next three days and I learned all sorts of stuff."

"And after that, you could get any girl you wanted?"

"No. I didn't kiss another girl until I was a junior in high school and that was during a game of Spin the Bottle. But once I got to college, my prospects improved. I was taller, the braces were off, I got contacts and a decent haircut. I was a film student, so I was considered cool without really having to work at it."

"I would have kissed you," Lily said. "I didn't get kissed until the night of my junior prom and then it was by Grady Perkins. And he was a horrible kisser, all wet and sloppy. I thought, 'If this is what everyone is talking about, then kissing is seriously overrated.'"

"Who gave you your first good kiss?" he asked.

"You did," Lily said. "When you kissed me on the plane as we were taking off. A kiss should be…surprising. And exhilarating and scary all at once. It should never be ordinary."

"For the woman who wrote *The Ten-Minute Seduction,* you're a real romantic."

Lily snuggled closer. "Sometimes I think that's just a reaction to what I watched my parents go through. I want to believe, but I know I'm being too idealistic."

"My parents have been married for thirty-five years," Aidan said. "They're still madly in love with each other."

"They're lucky," Lily said. She drew a deep breath, then dropped a quick kiss on his lips. "I need to figure out this wardrobe thing. And then I have to call Miranda and talk to her about the publicity tour."

"All right. But I want to make some plans for tonight," he said. "We're going to take the train into the city and see the ballgame. It'll be a date. And I'll even buy you supper."

"All right," Lily said, nodding. "It's a date."

Aidan rolled off the bed, then pointed to a pale green dress with an empire waist. "That one," he said. "It goes with your eyes." He grabbed his magazine from the floor and strolled out of the room.

Lily picked up the dress and held it to her body, staring at her reflection in the mirror. He was right. It did go with her eyes. Sometimes it seemed as though Aidan knew more about her than she did about herself. Though she hadn't meant to open herself so completely to this man, it had happened anyway. And Lily suspected she was in a lot deeper than she'd ever planned.

"I'VE NEVER been to a baseball game before," Lily said. "I've seen them on television and they look interesting."

She stood next to Aidan, clutching the overhead rail as the train rocked back and forth. He held on to her waist. To a casual observer it might seem a protective gesture, but in truth, Aidan liked to touch her, to maintain physical contact with her. If he couldn't hold her hand, then he rested his palm in the small of her back or held on to her elbow as she walked.

He'd seen his father do the same for years and he'd always thought it odd that his dad didn't trust his mother to stay upright on her own. But now, Aidan realized it had nothing to do with preventing a fall. His father just liked to touch Aidan's mother.

"You're not a big sports fan, I take it?"

"Miranda is more of a ballet-opera-symphony kind of person. And we always go to Broadway shows when we're here in the summer."

"We could go to a show," Aidan suggested. "It's not too late." In truth, Aidan had made some plans that Lily wasn't aware of and he wasn't sure how they'd go over.

"No, no. We're on a date. You should choose. And I'm interested in baseball. But I thought the team in New York was called the Yankees."

"New York has two teams," Aidan explained. "The Yankees and the Mets. Yankee Stadium is in the Bronx and Shea Stadium is in Flushing, in Queens. I grew up in Rockaway Beach in Queens. So I'm a Mets fan."

"Do your parents still live there?"

"In the same house. My mom is a schoolteacher and my dad works for the parks department."

She seemed surprised. "Wow, you do come from the All-American family," Lily said.

"Yep, that's me, All-American boy."

"It must have been nice to have a normal childhood. With normal memories. I think if I ever had children,

I'd want that for them. The whole celebrity thing is really confusing to a child. I never understood it."

"How is that?" Aidan asked.

"People were so interested in my parents. Complete strangers. Everywhere we went, they'd ask my mother for her autograph and they'd snap pictures. And the more out of control the marriage got, the more the photographers used to come after us. She'd have to dress up in a disguise just to take me to school."

"But your mother could have handled that differently, don't you think?"

Lily shrugged. "It was part of the job, she always said. A movie star is washed up when they don't want to take her picture anymore." She glanced out the window of the train. "This is normal, going to a baseball game on a train. There won't be any red carpet, no flashbulbs, no limousines. We can eat hot dogs and popcorn and you can buy me one of those baseball things and nobody will be following us."

"You want a foam finger?" Aidan asked.

"No, one of those…pennants. I'd like a pennant."

"I think I can do that for you. And maybe get you a cap, too. Get you indoctrinated properly. I wouldn't want you going over to the other side. The Yankees have enough fans."

The train station was right outside Shea Stadium. When the train pulled to a stop, Aidan stood behind Lily, holding tightly to her waist and keeping the crowd from trampling over her. He held on to her hand as they wove through the crush of spectators waiting to pass through the gates.

"This is exciting," Lily said, looking around in wonder. "Are we going to sit up high?"

"No, we have tickets on the third-base side," he said. "With some friends." He paused, wincing slightly. "Actually, we're going to be sitting with my folks."

Lily stopped short. "We're meeting your parents?"

Aidan turned to her. "I know, I probably should have told you earlier, but then, I didn't want to make a big deal out of it. Because it isn't a big deal. It's just a ball game. I gave my dad four season tickets for Christmas and no one else was using the extra two. Don't worry. I said I was bringing a friend. I didn't say girlfriend."

Lily stared down at the pretty cotton dress she wore. "Don't you think they're going to notice I'm a girl?"

"Yeah, but they won't automatically assume that you and I are sleeping together."

"We are sleeping together!" Lily shouted.

The crowd around them stopped to stare and a pretty pink blush colored her cheeks. "This is why I didn't tell you. Because I thought you'd take it the wrong way. We're just going to a ball game and my parents will be sitting next to us. They like baseball. They're nice people, Lily. You'll like them, I promise."

In truth, he wanted to introduce Lily to his parents. He wanted them to know he could meet a girl that they'd like, a regular girl, not one of those Hollywood types. And he wanted to show Lily that sometimes marriages did last forever, that there were couples that truly lived happily ever after.

"This is not fair," she protested, a stubborn set to her jaw. "You should have warned me."

"They're not radioactive," he said. "They aren't cannibals or ax murderers. They won't kidnap you and hold you for ransom. At the most, my mother might tell you you're pretty and my father might ask you if you'd like a beer. If that's cause for any concern, then we can just turn around and go back home."

It took Lily only a few moments to see the silliness of her fears. When she finally relented, he bent close and kissed her. "All right. We can go now."

Though the crowd was thick, Aidan spotted his parents right away. He waved, but they didn't see him until he and Lily were nearly standing in front of them. "Hi," he said.

They both turned, startled at first. Then his mother smiled broadly and gave him a hug. "There you are!" She reached up and rubbed his face. "I was expecting a beard like last time."

"Nope," he said. "No beard."

Aidan's father gave him a hug, clapping him on the back. "You look good. You got some sun."

Lily hung back, but Aidan turned around and grabbed her hand. "Mom, Dad, this is Lily Hart. Lily, this is my dad, Dan Pierce, and my mom, Ann Marie."

Lily smiled warmly and held out her hand. "Hello. It's a pleasure to meet you."

Aidan's mother drew her into a friendly hug. "Lily? Well, when Aidan said he'd be bringing a friend, I thought he'd show up with one of his old buddies from the neighborhood. I'm glad to see he's brought someone far more interesting." She linked her arm through Lily's and began to stroll toward the entrance. "How long have you two known each other?"

Aidan stood next to his father. "Pretty girl," his father said.

"She is," Aidan replied. "Smart, too."

"Is this something serious?" he asked.

Aidan shrugged. "I'm not sure yet. Maybe."

"Well, don't let your mother scare her off. She's been waiting for this day for a long time. Once she's got Lily cornered, I'm not sure Ann Marie is going to want to let her go. She might decide to lock her up in the basement and feed her chicken salad. Whenever we have company, she makes chicken salad. I've never quite understood that."

Aidan chuckled, recalling his words to Lily. He'd assured her that his parents posed no danger, but maybe he been too optimistic. "I'll make sure I sit between them."

Aidan found that trying to subvert his mother's interest in Lily was more difficult than he expected. She insisted Lily sit next to her. Rather than make a scene, Aidan gave in. But it was clear Ann Marie Pierce saw Lily as a potential mate for her bachelor son and she planned to fully evaluate her before the seventh-inning stretch.

After just a half inning, Aidan grabbed Lily's hand and pulled her to her feet. "Come on, let's go get you that cap I promised." He glanced over at his parents. "Can I bring you anything? Peanuts? Another beer? Lily and I are going shopping."

Ann Marie laughed. "Well, that's certainly a change for the better," she said. "Aidan used to hate shopping."

"We're going to buy a baseball cap, Mom, not new kitchen towels. We'll be right back."

He pulled Lily along toward the exit. Once they'd reached the concourse, Aidan grabbed her around the waist and drew her into a long, deep kiss. "I'm sorry," he said. "I'm sorry, I'm sorry. I didn't think she'd be like this."

"Like what?" Lily asked. "Your mother is very nice."

"Nice? I'd call that overbearing. She's interrogating you. She asked you what you liked to eat for dinner. And it's not even the second inning. She's already planning some big family event that'll include you. I'm sure she'll invite all the relatives and there will be photos. She'll lure you in with food, massive quantities of food."

"Has she done this before?" Lily asked, laughing. "Are any of your old girlfriends buried in the backyard?"

"No. I've never brought a girl home before. And this is why."

"But you've introduced girls to your parents."

He shook his head. "Not since high school. And those were only friends."

Lily stared at him in disbelief. "Is it any wonder your mother is interested in talking to me? She probably thought you were gay."

Aidan frowned, seeing the sense in Lily's words. "Oh, well now that makes sense," he murmured. "Not that my parents would have a problem with that. But that's not why I haven't brought a girl home. Most of the girls I've been with lately haven't been the type to appreciate Rockaway Beach."

"And you thought I would?"

Aidan shrugged. "I knew it wouldn't make a difference to you. Lily, you're the most unpretentious person I've ever known. And you're funny and sweet and I wanted my parents to know I could find someone that they'd approve of. I'm sorry if I put you on the spot. I didn't mean to. But I knew you wouldn't read any deep meaning into this. It's just a ball game."

Lily pushed up on her toes and gave him a kiss. "Don't worry. I can handle your mother. You forget, I live with Miranda Sinclair. She's certifiably crazy and I manage to keep her in line. Your mother is an amateur compared to my scary godmother." Lily chuckled. "Wait till Miranda gets hold of you. She'll tie you to a chair, shine a light in your eyes and ask you to recount every woman you've ever slept with. And she loves juicy details."

Aidan smiled. He looked forward to meeting Miranda face-to-face. He wanted to tell her how wonderful her goddaughter was and how much he cared for Lily and how thankful he was she hadn't taken that flight. He wanted to believe he and Lily would go through all those days that couples went through on their way to a life together. "I think I can handle Miranda. I've talked to her on the phone a few times and she doesn't seem that bad."

"Yeah, but you hadn't slept with me then."

"She's the one who set this thing up," Aidan said.

"If it weren't for her, we wouldn't have been on that plane together."

"We'll have to find a way to thank her," Lily said. "Maybe we should buy her a foam finger."

"LILY! Lily, where are you?"

Lily glanced up from the computer at the sound of Aidan's voice. "I'm back here. In the office."

Aidan had gone into town to pick up his airline ticket from a local travel agent. And Lily had spent the morning trying to revise the third chapter of her novel, hoping that work might help her forget the fact that he was leaving the next day. She'd known it was coming. They both seemed to be preparing themselves to say goodbye by acting as though it was an ordinary occurrence, simple and unemotional.

She bit her bottom lip and fought back a surge of tears. The last five days had been the most exciting, most romantic of her life. Every fantasy she'd ever imagined had come true, and now it was almost over.

"What are you doing?"

"Working," Lily said, forcing a smile. "Did you get your ticket?"

Aidan nodded. He crossed the room, then braced his hands on the arms of her chair and gave her a quick kiss. "All set. I have to be at the airport at 6:00 a.m. tomorrow morning. What are you working on?"

Lily reached out to close the document, but Aidan stopped her. "It's just a book," she explained.

"Another Lacey St. Claire how-to?"

She shook her head. "No. It's a novel. Kind of the story of my life, but not. It's just…nothing. Not yet."

"Can I read it?"

Lily shook her head. "No. It's not done."

"Would it make a good movie?" he asked.

She shrugged. "I don't know. It's kind of funny, I think. It's about a child of Hollywood and her very dysfunctional family."

"A comedy? I've never directed a comedy," he said, his interest piqued. "When it's done, will you let me read it?"

Lily nodded. They'd already made so many little promises about the future, one more wouldn't make a difference. Besides, it might be nice to have his opinion. She certainly respected his taste. "I will," she said.

"Good." He grabbed her hand and pulled her out of her chair. "Come on, I brought lunch home. Why don't we eat and then we can spend the afternoon lying around next to the pool, trying to talk each other into skinny-dipping."

He caught her around the waist, walking behind her as they headed out to the kitchen. When she got there, she found bags from the local deli—and a brand-new copy of *The Ten-Minute Seduction.* Lily held it up. "What's this?"

"I bought a copy at the bookstore in town. I thought you might sign it for me. I needed something to read on the plane."

"No!" Lily cried. "You can't read this on the plane."

"Why not?"

"Because it might give you ideas. I don't want you to end up in the bathroom with some horny passenger."

"Ah, jealousy rears its ugly head," he teased, tweaking the end of her nose. He grabbed one of the bags and spread the contents on the counter. "You do like me, don't you?"

Lily peeked into the other bag to find plastic containers full of cold salads. "I've had fun these last few days," she murmured. "And I'm sorry it's going to be over."

"So what are we going to do about it?" Aidan asked.

She picked up a container of potato salad and stared at the label. The question was just waiting to be asked and Lily swore to herself she wasn't going to be the first to ask it. But she needed to know the answer.

"We could make plans to see each other again," she murmured. The words were out of her mouth before she could stop them.

He took the potato salad from her hand and opened it, then handed it back to her with a plastic fork. "I was just thinking about that. I'm going to be in L.A. for about a week. But I could come back here when I'm finished."

"I'm not going to be here," Lily said. "The publicity tour starts out in Florida at the end of next week and then I go to Texas. I'll be back here in three weeks for a little break, though. We could meet then."

"All right. Three weeks," he said. "I'll plan to come back in three weeks."

Lily nodded. Now that they'd actually put together future plans, the pain that had settled around her heart had suddenly lifted. Three weeks wasn't so long. She could wait.

"And we'll talk," Aidan said. "I have your cell phone on my memory dial, so I won't forget it."

"We will talk," Lily said.

He nodded. "All right. I'm glad we have that taken care of. Now, I'm going to go change into some shorts and then we can eat out by the pool."

Lily nodded, watching as he jogged out the back door toward the pool house. Over the past few days, she'd tried to memorize all the little details that she loved about him. The exact shade of his eyes, the dimple in his left cheek, the way his lips curled into a smile when he was amused. She'd studied his body and the way it moved, watched his hands as he spoke. There was so much to take in, so much that she found intriguing about him.

Lily heard her cell phone ring and she grabbed her purse from the counter and pulled it out. Aidan's name showed up on the caller ID. Frowning, she flipped open the phone. "What do you want?"

"I'm just making sure this works," he said. "I miss you."

"We've only been apart for less than a minute," Lily said. "And if I stand at the kitchen door, I can probably see you."

"I know. But it seems like five or ten minutes. The time just goes so slowly when you're not here."

"What are you doing?" Lily asked as she picked through the things he'd purchased from the deli. There were times when Aidan could be such a tease. "Just come back and help me with lunch."

"I'm undressing," he said. "What are you wearing?"

"Clothes," she said. "You just saw me. I'm wearing a blue dress."

"No, that's not the way it goes. You're supposed to tell me you're naked. Or you're wearing something really sexy."

"I am?"

"Yeah. Since we're going to be apart for a while, I think we should practice having phone sex," Aidan explained.

"Why would we do that when we're still living in the same house?"

"Because if it doesn't go well then I can come up to your bedroom and we can have real sex."

Lily giggled. "I'm not sure I can do this," she said.

"Sure you can. First, you have to go up to your bedroom and take off all your clothes. And you have to tell me about it while you're doing it."

"No!"

"Come on, Lily. It'll be fun. I promise. And what are you going to do with yourself all alone in those hotel rooms in Florida and Texas? I don't want to have sex with anyone else. So, it's either the phone or nothing."

"Have you ever heard of self-gratification?" Lily asked. "I hear men enjoy that on occasion."

"Yeah, but it's much more fun if I enjoy that with you on the other end of the phone talking dirty to me."

Lily sat down on a kitchen stool and opened up a bottle of ginger ale. "All right," she murmured. "I'm walking to my bedroom right now. I'm unbuttoning my dress."

"What are you wearing underneath?" he asked.

"Nothing," she said. "I didn't put any underwear on this morning. It didn't think I'd need it."

He moaned softly. "I wish you'd told me that when I was in the kitchen."

"What are you wearing?" she asked.

"Nothing. I'm lying on the bed wearing nothing. And I'm thinking about this morning, when you were in this bed with me. I'm thinking about what we did together."

Lily smiled to herself as images of their lovemaking drifted through her mind. "Do you remember how I touched you?" she asked. "Why don't you touch yourself just like that and tell me how it feels?" She bit her bottom lip to keep from giggling. Though it was a little odd to be talking like this, Lily could see how it might relieve stress. But it was certainly no substitute for real sex.

"All right," he said. "I'm doing that. Tell me what you're doing."

She took a bite of the potato salad. "I'm lying on my bed and I'm touching myself." She sighed. "Oh, that feels so good."

"Tell me more," he said, his voice low. "Tell me what you'd do to me if we were together."

Lily felt herself growing warm. Though talking like this was a bit embarrassing, she had to admit, it was also very liberating. Very Lacey St. Claire. "I'd start kissing you," she said. "Little kisses at first. Along your neck, down your chest. To that little trail of hair below your belly button. And then lower."

"Where?"

"You know where," she said. "I'd kiss you there. And run my tongue all over you. And when you couldn't stand it anymore, I'd—"

"You are such a liar!"

Lily spun around to see Aidan standing in the door, grinning, his phone pressed to his ear. He'd changed into board shorts, but it was obvious from the bulge in front that their conversation had worked. He was definitely aroused.

"So are you!" she accused, jumping off the stool.

"You're supposed to be naked."

"So are you," she said.

They stared at each other, caught in a silly challenge. Then Aidan shrugged and skimmed his shorts down, revealing his arousal. Lily reached for the hem of her skirt and tugged the dress over her head, tossing it aside.

"Are you happy now?" she asked.

"Very," he murmured.

"Luisa is going to be back in a few minutes. She just went grocery shopping," Lily warned.

"Maybe you could give her the afternoon off."

Lily crossed the kitchen and stood in front of him. She glanced down at his erection and smiled. "Did you miss me?"

With a low growl, Aidan grabbed her waist and picked her up off her feet. He carried her out to the pool, Lily wriggling in his arms. "No, I don't want to get wet," she cried.

But Aidan didn't listen. He carried her to the deep end

and then jumped off the side. The water was cold at first and Lily gasped before they both sank below the surface.

She'd miss the romance and she'd miss the sex. But being with Aidan was also a lot of fun. Of all the things she'd miss, Lily knew she'd miss that the most.

8

LILY STARED at Aidan's profile, outlined by the moonlight streaming through the French doors of her bedroom. They lay amidst the remains of their lovemaking, discarded clothes, tangled sheets and the scents of her perfume and his shampoo mixing with the salty sea breeze.

Every time they made love, it was a revelation. Lily discovered new facets of her desire, new ways to please him and new sensations that raced through her body at his touch. She wondered how long they might go on like this, had the outside world not intruded.

She closed her eyes and imagined them both stranded on a tropical island with nothing to do all day but enjoy each other. They'd swim and lie in the sun and nap when they'd exhausted themselves making love. That's what this week had been to her, a deserted island, a fantasy vacation.

She glanced over at the clock on her bedside table. It was 2:00 a.m. The car was due to pick him up in another three hours for the ride to JFK. She'd offered to drive him into the city, but he'd insisted he could hire a car.

In truth, Lily was glad. She knew saying goodbye would be difficult enough. She didn't want to do it at the terminal, with people milling about and the police yelling at her to move out of the loading zone. This would be much better, just to kiss him and watch him walk out. But until then, she didn't want to close her eyes.

Though Lily had avoided facing her feelings, she knew she'd fallen in love with Aidan. This wasn't the same infatuation she'd felt since first setting eyes on him. She'd created him out of her imagination and had thought that's what she'd wanted. But the real Aidan was so much more than the man she imagined him to be.

It was as if they already had a past. Lily couldn't find another way to describe the easy give-and-take between them. He seemed to read her moods and respond in exactly the right way, with a word or a touch or a look that made all her insecurities disappear.

How had this happened? She'd tried so hard to maintain a safe distance. Lily knew the risks of falling in love. And yet, he'd wriggled his way into her heart, he'd possessed her body and kidnapped her soul. And nothing she could tell herself would make his leaving any easier.

She reached out to touch him, ready to wake him and beg him to stay. But her fingers hovered over his shoulder, feeling the heat from his body. Separation might be good for them, she told herself. It would test the depth and strength of their feelings. Besides, any relationship with Aidan would require long absences.

Maybe it was best to find out how she'd handle them before she professed her love.

Why was it so hard for her to say those words? Was it because they'd never really meant anything to her? Her mother had always thrown them around, to friends, to fans, to Lily. *I love you.* How was she supposed to believe when it had been so easy for her parents to walk away? They were supposed to love her and yet they'd left her behind.

Tears welled in her eyes. In all the years she'd lived with Miranda, she'd never said those words to her godmother. And though Miranda used the words sparingly, Lily knew her godmother loved her.

"I love you," she whispered. "I love you, Aidan."

She felt the ache deep inside her and for the first time, Lily found the meaning in the sentiment. But it was easy to say the words when they went unheard. It would be much more difficult looking into Aidan's eyes and knowing the feeling wasn't returned.

Lily drew the covers back, taking care not to wake Aidan. Grabbing a robe from the floor, she pulled it over her naked body, then slipped from the bedroom. She found her phone where she had left it that afternoon, on the kitchen counter.

Grabbing it, she wandered into the family room. She curled up in an overstuffed chair, tucking her feet beneath her, then dialed Miranda's number.

"Hi. It's me," she said when Miranda picked up.

"Lily. What time is it there?"

"It's late," Lily said. "Or maybe it's early. I'm not sure."

"Is everything all right?"

She drew a ragged breath, gathering her resolve. She wouldn't allow herself to cry. "I just wanted to thank you. I know I was pretty harsh on the phone earlier this week, but I want you to know I appreciate everything you do for me."

"Now I know there's something wrong," Miranda said, worry evident in the tone of her voice.

"No, no. Everything is good. For once, all your scheming worked. He's wonderful. He's everything I've ever wanted."

"So why do you sound so sad?"

"I—I guess I'm just not ready to deal with the realities of a relationship," Lily said. "I kind of liked the fantasies. Nothing bad ever happened."

"Lily, just because things get difficult, it doesn't mean they're going to fall apart altogether. You just have to work a little harder."

"Like my parents did?" Lily asked.

A long silence spun across the distance between them. "Let me tell you something about your parents. They were not a good match from the start. I loved your mother. She was my best friend, the first person I really got to know when I moved to L.A. And I told her not to marry your father, but she was stubborn and she was certain she could make him settle down. It wasn't all bad, Lily."

"You forget. I lived through it."

"They did one good thing in that marriage. They had you. And you grew up to be a beautiful, talented, passionate woman. So, I guess you can't say their marriage was a complete failure."

"Were they ever in love?"

"Of course. But your mother was young and very idealistic. And your father was used to having any woman he wanted. You don't have to make the same mistakes, Lily. That was their life. You need to live your own."

"When are you coming out here?" Lily asked.

"In a few days," Miranda said.

"Could you come soon?" Lily asked. "You could catch the red-eye tonight and I could pick you up at the airport. Everything is ready here. And I'd like to spend a few days with you before I have to start the publicity tour."

"I could help you get ready for the talk show," Miranda suggested.

"I'd like that." Lily sighed softly. "I should go. Call me and let me know your flight number."

"Tell him how you feel, Lily. Don't let him leave without telling him."

"I don't know how I feel."

"Yes, you do. You're just afraid to admit it."

Another silence passed between them. "I love you, Miranda. I don't think I've ever told you how grateful I am for everything that you've done over the years. You're the mother I should have had."

"I love you, too, Lily. Sleep tight." The other end of the line went dead and Lily closed her eyes and tipped her head back, the tears running freely down her cheeks. Lily brushed them away, trying to bring her emotions under control.

In the end, she allowed herself to cry. She cried for everything that had ever hurt her, for all the pain she'd kept so tightly in check over the years. And in the end, it left her exhausted.

When she crawled back into bed with Aidan, she thought she might sleep. But instead, Lily smoothed her hand over his handsome face and kissed him. Slowly, he awoke, becoming aware of her naked body next to his.

His hand slipped around her waist and he pulled her closer. Without speaking, he returned her kiss. Lily closed her eyes and let herself float on the wave of desire that swirled around her. His hands explored her body and his mouth teased at the places that only he knew.

"Make love to me," she murmured, raking her fingers through his hair. "Make love to me."

And when he finally entered her, Lily felt complete. This was her life, here with this man. Was she brave enough to reach out and grab happiness where she'd found it? Or would she let her fear of abandonment destroy any chance she had with Aidan?

HE DIDN'T need an alarm clock to wake him. Aidan had been awake since Lily had disturbed his sleep with her kiss. He'd made love to her in a hazy world of exhaustion and excitement, a desperate escape from what they knew was coming.

His bags were packed and sitting next to the front door. The car was due in a few minutes. He'd spent the last half hour trying to decide whether to wake Lily and say goodbye or let her sleep. He wasn't sure what to expect from her.

He wanted her to cry and beg him to stay, to profess her feelings for him. Aidan knew if she did that, he'd be lost. But if she merely kissed him and waved goodbye, that would be even more painful.

They'd played this game from the start and now Aidan wanted it to end. They'd pretended what they shared was merely fueled by physical desire and not emotion. But there was no denying he'd grown fond of Lily. More than fond, he thought. If he didn't know what love was, then he'd guess this was pretty close.

But they'd spent just six days together. How was that enough time to fall in love? Though love at first sight was a popular movie concept, Aidan could never see the possibility. Love was supposed to take work, it was supposed to be nurtured. It wasn't supposed to just fall out of the sky and drop at his feet.

At least they'd discussed a future of sorts. They'd see each other again in three weeks. Maybe after some time apart he'd have a better handle on his feelings. He wanted to know for sure before he said anything.

Aidan pressed a gentle kiss to her forehead, then drew a deep breath, committing the scent of her hair to memory. He crawled out of her bed and picked up the clothes he'd laid out to wear on the plane, oddly, the same thing he'd been wearing when he met Lily.

It was a strange circle he'd just completed. Their first encounter on the plane seemed as though it had happened years ago. In just six days, he and Lily had spent a lifetime together. He'd never known a woman so intimately nor had he allowed any woman to know him.

Maybe it was the nature of a vacation romance. It was easy to be honest because the relationship had an end in sight. And maybe that's what had given him permission finally to let down his guard and consider the possibility of falling in love.

He tugged his boxers over his hips, then stepped into his cargo pants. Luisa had washed and ironed his shirt and he stared at Lily as he buttoned it up.

How close had they come to walking away from each other that day at the Hartford airport? Had she felt the attraction as deeply as he had? When she'd turned to ask if he'd come with her to the Hamptons, it was almost as if destiny had taken a hand.

The first light of dawn illuminated the room and he glanced again at the clock, mentally counting down the minutes until he had to walk away. Staring at his reflection in the mirror above the dresser, Aidan raked his hands through his hair.

He'd thought about taking a shower, but he wanted the scent of her on his body for as long as possible. Aidan smiled to himself. God, it was so strange that something as insignificant as that would be important to him now. Everything was important—the sound of her voice, the feel of her hand in his, the way she said his name. He'd come to know all those things so well.

Once he'd found his shoes, Aidan knew he was ready. But he wanted to leave a note for Lily, something to let her know he was thinking about her. He glanced around the room, searching for a piece of paper, and found a stack beneath a magazine next to the bed. But when he picked it up, Aidan realized it was a manuscript. Stepping closer to the window, he read the first page, and then the second and the third.

Though the excerpt came from the middle of the book, Aidan found himself captivated by the writing style. She was describing a simple haircut for a child at a high-style Hollywood salon. The characters were outrageously self-absorbed and the child narrating the story possessed a wicked wit.

He wanted to take the pages with him, but Lily had refused to let him read what she'd written. Going against her wishes would be a betrayal of her trust. Aidan made a mental note to ask her about the manuscript when he saw her the next time.

Aidan walked back to the bed and picked up his watch and cell phone from the nightstand. Staring down at her, he flipped open the phone and dialed her number. He heard her phone ring from somewhere in the house. When her voice mail picked up, he spoke softly.

"Hi," he said. "It's time for me to go and I'm standing here looking at you and wondering what the hell I'm doing. I want to crawl back into bed with you and stay there for another week. But I have business to do and so do you. So, rather than wake you, I'm going to go now. Know that I'm thinking about you, and about how lucky I was to meet you on that plane. I'll talk to you soon. Take care, Lily."

He slowly closed the phone, then drew a deep breath. Fighting the temptation to bend over and kiss her, Aidan turned away from the bed. If he kissed her, she might wake up. And if she woke up, he might want to do more than kiss her. And if that happened, he'd never leave.

Aidan walked to the door, then took one last look at Lily before heading to the front of the house. "I'll see you soon," he murmured.

As he walked out into the damp morning air, he wondered what it would be like the next time they saw each other. Would the attraction still be as intense or would it have cooled? Would they pick up where they'd left off or would they have to get to know each other again? These were all questions that worried him, but he knew they'd figure out a way to get through the confusion and back to where they belonged.

The driver stepped out of the car and opened the back door. Aidan tossed his bag inside, then looked back at the house, shrouded in an early-morning fog. He smiled as he remembered the day they'd arrived. So many things had changed in such a short time. He wouldn't have thought it possible.

"JFK?" the driver asked.

Aidan nodded. He got inside, then leaned back into the soft leather seat, closing his eyes and tipping his head back.

As the car pulled out of the long driveway and Aidan felt the distance between himself and Lily growing, he wanted to tell the driver to turn around and go back. To hell with his meetings, to hell with his career. But it wasn't business that was taking him away. If this strange new thing they called a relationship was going to last in the real world, then they had to give it a chance.

He'd be back, they'd see each other again, and no doubt, things wouldn't go as planned. But he was ready for the challenges. For the first time in his life, he'd found a woman worth fighting for.

"MISS ST. CLAIRE, we're ready for you in hair and makeup. If you'll come with me, I'll take you."

Lily stared at the page of the magazine she was trying to read, her mind spinning with the questions and answers she'd so carefully practiced.

"Miss St. Claire?"

Lily glanced up to see the assistant producer of *Talk to Me* standing in the door of the green room. "I'm sorry." Though she knew she was Miss St. Claire now, Lily still had a hard time answering to the name. She stood and smoothed her hands over the front of her dress. "Miranda was here just a minute ago. Have you seen her?"

"She's down in makeup chatting with Gail."

Gail was Gail Weatherby, one of four hosts on *Talk to Me*. Gail was the most seasoned journalist of the group and would be doing the interview with occasional questions from the others. The assistant producer had gone over many of the questions with Lily, but had warned her that there might be some unexpected inquiries.

No matter what happened, she was to keep the interview light and humorous and not take any of the questions too seriously. The problem was, Lily didn't feel very funny at the moment. In fact, she felt as though she was about to lose the doughnut she'd just eaten for breakfast.

"Do you think this dress is all right?" Lily asked.

"Oh, it's perfect," the assistant producer said. "The color brings out your eyes. And the neckline frames your face beautifully. You couldn't have picked anything better for television."

"I—I didn't pick it," Lily said. "My—my boyfriend did. I mean, he's really just a friend. Although we are romantically involved. But I wouldn't call him my—"

"You'll be fine," the producer said, patting her on the arm. "Just relax and be yourself."

That was the problem. They expected her to relax and be Lacey St. Claire. But she wasn't Lacey St. Claire. The last time she'd been Lacey St. Claire was the night before Aidan had left for L.A. Since then, she'd been feeling more and more like the old Lily Hart.

When she stepped inside the makeup room, she found Miranda relaxing in one of the chairs while Gail was getting her hair done. Miranda had been on the show two or three times and was doing her usual job of charming everyone around her, which was amazing, since just an hour ago, she had been dishing the dirt with Lily on all four of the cohosts, from their plastic surgeries to their extramarital affairs.

"Darling," Miranda cried. "There you are. I was just telling Gail all about the runaway success of this book. I knew it the moment I read the book," she gushed, turning back to Gail. "It was important. It was… What's the word you used, Lily?"

"Liberating?"

"Yes, yes. Liberating. Even though we're all mature women, we still have our little hang-ups about sex. We stand on equal ground in the work place. It's about time we stood on the same ground in the bedroom." Miranda paused. "Of course, those are Lily's words. She was just saying that to me yesterday, weren't you, darling?"

Those words had never come out of Lily's mouth. If they had, she certainly would have been a much more interesting person to talk to. "Where should I sit?" Lily asked.

Miranda stood. "Here, darling. You sit here and chat with Gail. I'm going to go get a cup of coffee."

Lily looked at Gail in the mirror and smiled. "She's something, isn't she?"

"Your godmother is quite a woman," Gail said. "I would expect she could be difficult to live with though."

Lily shook her head. "Not really." She wasn't about to say anything that could be twisted and discussed on the air. Miranda had warned her to watch out for Gail. Though she was the host of a women's talk show, she wasn't afraid to ask probing questions.

"Miranda says that you've been dating a movie director. Aidan Pierce?"

"We're not dating," Lily said. "We're just friends. Good friends. I think Miranda likes to…embellish my love life."

"But your love life is probably quite interesting, considering the subject matter of your book," Gail said.

Lily opened her mouth, then closed it, considering her answer carefully. "I feel like the interview has started already," she murmured.

"I'm just trying to get a feel for you," Gail said. "Sometimes these little chats bring up interesting subjects to discuss. Did Miranda help you at all with the book?"

Lily nodded. "She suggested the premise behind it. She read all the drafts and then she sent it to her publisher—without my knowledge. She really encouraged me."

"So tell me how you met Aidan Pierce. My producer said he's really hot."

Lily laughed lightly. "We're just friends. I swear."

A knock sounded on the door and they both turned. The associate producer was standing there holding a huge bouquet of flowers. "These just came for you," she said.

"Oh, put them over there," Gail replied.

"No, they came for Lacey St. Claire." She set them down on the counter in front of Lily. "There's a card."

Lily plucked the card out of the greenery. "Leave it to Miranda. She's always been one for big gestures." She opened the card and read silently. *Break a leg, Lily. Love, Aidan.*

Lily folded the card and slipped it back into the envelope. Then, leaning forward, she took a deep breath, letting the scent of the summer bouquet fill her head.

Over the past few days, she'd received all sorts of little gifts, some delivered by overnight mail, some just arriving at the house in the Hamptons. Aidan had sent

her a book on the lighthouses of Long Island and he'd
sent her a photo of himself standing next to the teapot
he'd bought at the antique store. He'd sent her a box of
chocolate truffles from one of the best chocolatiers in
Manhattan. Just yesterday, a Mets jersey had arrived
along with a silly card.

A few moments later, Miranda came sweeping into
the room, two paper cups of coffee in her hands. "I had
to send someone out for these. Oh my, what lovely
flowers. Gail, do you have a secret admirer?"

"They're Lily's," Gail said.

"They're lovely. Another gift from Aidan, I'd assume?"

Gail's eyebrow shot up. "I thought you said you were
just friends."

"We are," Lily assured her. "He just sent them for luck."

Gail gave her hair a critical look, then nodded. "All
right. I have to get ready. Lily—or should I say, Lacey—
I'll see you on set. Miranda, as always, it's been a
pleasure. Call me and we'll have lunch. I have a charity
auction I'd love for you to attend."

Miranda watched as Lily got her hair and makeup
done, making suggestions along the way and involving
herself in a heated discussion of Lily's lipstick color. In
the end, Miranda won out and the makeup person
wandered away in defeat.

"You have to be very firm with these people," Miranda
said. "It's your image at stake here. If you don't like
something, just speak up. Remember, you're the one in
charge. You make the demands and they meet them. If
you show any weakness at all, they'll take advantage."

"I understand," Lily said softly. She pulled the card out and read it again. *Love, Aidan*. The other cards had been signed in other ways. This was the first time he'd used the word *love*.

Lily sighed. What was she doing? Once again she was creating a fantasy that didn't exist. In a few weeks, she'd see him again and they'd pick up where they left off. There would still be things left unsaid between them, still the same doubts and insecurities. But imagining that he was in love with her, and building a simple word into a huge fantasy, would be a mistake.

"What is this?" Miranda said.

Lily glanced up at her reflection in the mirror. "What?"

"This face. Good God, Lily, you look so…so glum. Smile. I'm tired of this sad face all day long."

"Don't tell me how I'm supposed to feel," Lily snapped. "I've spent my whole life denying the fact that I felt anything. If I want to be glum, I can be glum."

"So I was right? The flowers are from him?" Miranda asked. "Well, at least he's considerate, I'll give him that."

"He's more than considerate," Lily said. "He's— he's wonderful."

"Then you should be dancing around the room. But instead, you're thinking about all the things that can go wrong. You're worrying about the next time you see each other or whether you'll see each other again at all."

Miranda knew her too well. "I can't help it."

"Yes, you can. You can start to believe you deserve good things in your life, especially a good man." She sighed. "By the way, I asked my real estate agent to start looking for a house for you. I know you've been saving and with the money from the book, you should be in a position to buy."

Lily stared at Miranda, stunned by the revelation. "I thought you'd be upset."

"Darling, we can't have this man sneaking over to sleep with you at my house. It just wouldn't be seemly. You need your own space. But I want to make sure you find a nice place, somewhere close by. So I've decided to make you a little loan." She held up her hand, refusing to hear any further discussion. "We'll discuss this after you return from your book tour."

Miranda pushed out of the chair and walked to the door. "Where is this man right now?"

"He's in L.A.," Lily said.

"You have two days before you leave for your tour. Get on a plane and go see him." Miranda turned on her heel and walked away, leaving Lily to her thoughts.

Miranda was right. There was nothing stopping her from spending her last few days of freedom in L.A. with Aidan. Though she hated flying, maybe it wouldn't be so bad if she knew she was traveling toward something wonderful. Lily grabbed her purse and searched through the contents for her cell phone. If she left right after her interview, she might be in L.A. by the evening. That would give her two nights with Aidan before she'd need to leave again.

She flipped open her phone and stared at the photo of himself that he'd sent her. It was difficult to think of him as a flesh-and-blood man when all she had was the photo and her memories.

Miranda was right. She had every reason to be optimistic. And a quick trip back to L.A. would do a lot to make her feel less…glum.

9

Six months later

AIDAN STARED at the sign in the bookstore window, set amidst the Christmas gift display. Lily looked different in the picture, not the same woman he'd known last summer. She was such a natural beauty, but in this photo she looked…too perfect. But then, he hadn't seen Lily in a long time. Why shouldn't she have changed?

He glanced up and down Coventry Street, watching as the Londoners hurried home through the damp and sleet. Aidan had been in England for a week, doing pre-production on a new film set during the Blitz of the Second World War. He'd been taking the time to absorb the atmosphere of the city between production meetings, walking the streets and searching for locations he wanted to use for the film. But since he'd learned Lily was going to be in town, he couldn't focus on anything else.

Aidan had never anticipated it would end so quietly. After only a few days apart, Lily had offered to fly back to L.A. for a visit, but by then, Aidan had agreed to make a quick trip to Japan to promote the Asian release of his last film. They'd both still been determined to make it work, but one schedule conflict after another had kept them apart throughout the rest of the summer.

After that, they never seemed to find a time when they both were free. Maybe they'd been too stubborn, not willing to settle for a day here or a short weekend there. They'd wanted a week, like they'd had in the Hamptons, a chance to really enjoy each other's company.

Throughout their first month apart, they talked each day. Then by August, the phone calls dwindled to a few times a week and they'd resigned themselves to the fact that a relationship wasn't going to be easy. Gradually, during the autumn, they managed a call every week or two, each conversation a bit more uncomfortable than the last as they both realized it might not ever work.

Though he hadn't talked to Lily in two months, Aidan had kept up with her publicity schedule on her Web page. The book had hit the bestseller lists in September and Lily's publicity tour had been extended when *The Ten-Minute Seduction* was published in England.

Now that they were finally going to be in the same city for a few nights, he'd decided an invitation to dinner might be appropriate. It was time to settle this between them once and for all.

They'd once agreed just to let it go, to avoid the fights and the regrets and a big, messy breakup, if they grew apart. But Aidan couldn't do that. It left too many doubts in his mind. He needed answers and he planned to get them.

Aidan knew how he felt. There wasn't a night that went by when he didn't think of Lily in the moments before he drifted off to sleep. And in the mornings, he woke up wondering what she had planned for her day. He hadn't been with another woman since Lily. Hell, he hadn't even thought about another woman, sexually or otherwise. Lily was the only one he wanted.

Aidan pulled open the door of the bookstore and stepped inside. There was a small crowd gathered near the back, but Aidan decided to evaluate the situation first. He wandered down a side aisle and scanned the books distractedly. He found a good vantage point near a small seating area and grabbed a book before sitting down.

Holding the volume in front of his face, he peered over the top and watched as the crowd moved. A moment later, he caught sight of Lily, sitting behind a table stacked with her seduction book, a pen in her hand.

She chatted with each person who handed her a copy, smiling graciously as she signed her name. God, he hadn't remembered how beautiful she was…or what the beauty could do to him. He felt an ache growing in the pit of his stomach. He didn't want to walk away again without knowing exactly where he stood with her, but he didn't want it all to end here, in this bookstore.

The line dwindled a bit and Aidan stood and walked over to the table. Lily was focused on the person in front of her and didn't see him. When he reached the front of the line, she grabbed a book and opened it in front of her without even looking at him.

"Make it out to Slave Boy," he said. "Actually, make that Slave Assistant."

Her gaze snapped up and she gasped. "Hi," she murmured, a look of disbelief on her pretty face. "What are you doing here?"

"I'm in London on business. I—I saw the sign and decided to come in." Best not to admit he'd been stalking her over the Internet. "Strange that we finally see each other again and it's in London."

"I know," she said. "It's been a while."

He nodded, shoving his hands into his jacket pockets. "It has. So, how did you get here? You must have conquered your fear of flying."

"I'm working on it," she said. "I figured it was about time to put that behind me. I'm still a little crazy at takeoff, but then I calm down."

"Listen, I know you're busy here. I just wanted to stop by and say hello."

"Hello," she murmured, a smile playing on her lips.

"Hello." He glanced over his shoulder to see the line growing behind him. "Would you like to get a cup of coffee after you're finished?"

Lily nodded. "I would. Where?"

"There's a coffee shop just a few doors down. Out the door and to the left. I'll meet you there."

"It's a date," she said.

"Yes, it is. Our second date, right?"

Lily nodded and Aidan slowly backed away, his gaze still fixed on her. He'd forgotten how easy it was to get lost in those beautiful green eyes. He could see all her emotions reflected there. And it was evident there was still an overwhelming attraction between them.

Aidan grinned as he walked back through the bookshop and out onto the busy street. Pulling his jacket tight against the damp and cold, he turned his face up to the night sky and whooped joyfully. The passing pedestrians gave him an odd look and a wide berth, but he didn't care. By the end of the night, he was going to have Lily back, in his arms and in his life.

Her book-signing was supposed to over by nine o'clock, but she didn't arrive at the coffee shop until nearly ten. Aidan was flipping through a day-old copy of the *New York Times* when she walked up to his table.

"Sorry. We had people lined up and I didn't want to send them away without an autograph."

Aidan got to his feet and pulled out a chair for her, then helped her out of her coat. For a brief moment, he let his hands linger on her shoulders, feeling the warmth beneath his fingertips. It had been so long since he touched her he'd forgotten how deeply it affected him.

When he sat down across from her, she was nervously fingering the menu. A waiter came over and Lily ordered a mocha latte, while Aidan ordered another coffee.

They chatted about her book tour and his new film, carefully avoiding any discussion of their interlude in the Hamptons. To a casual observer, they might have seemed like good friends or business acquaintances, not lovers.

Aidan grew tired of the small talk and when he reached across the table and grabbed her hand, Lily jumped, as if his touch had sent a shock through her.

"Are we going to say anything important here?" Aidan asked. "Or are we just going to avoid the subject?"

She stared down into her coffee mug. "I'm not sure what to say. I guess it didn't work out the way we'd planned."

"Why did we stop talking, Lily?"

"It just seemed easier," she said. "Every conversation was the same. We'd try to find a time to get away and there were always excuses and commitments."

"It's not supposed to be easy," Aidan countered. "But that doesn't mean we stop trying."

"I know. That's what Miranda told me." She took a deep breath. "I should go," Lily murmured. "I have to be up early tomorrow for an interview."

It was obvious she didn't want to talk about what had happened. She'd carefully avoided his gaze and Aidan could see the tears welling up in her eyes. "Can I see you tomorrow?" he asked. "Maybe we could go to dinner. I don't know anyone in London…except you."

"All right," Lily said. "I'm staying at the Kensington Park Hotel. Room 1155. Call me."

He stood. "Can I walk you back to your hotel?"

She shook her head. "I'll get a cab."

Aidan grabbed her hand and leaned toward her, dropping a kiss on her cheek. "It was good to see you."

"Yes. This was nice. Thank you for the coffee."

He watched her walk out of the shop, then sat down at their table. Hell, this was going to be a lot harder than he'd imagined. But he couldn't believe she wasn't experiencing the same sense of frustration and loss.

Why couldn't they just say what they felt? He was ready to tell her, but she'd almost sensed what was coming and cut him off. He couldn't let that happen again.

Aidan grabbed his wallet out of his pocket and threw a ten-pound note on the table to cover the check. He had from now until dinner tomorrow night to figure out how to get Lily Hart back into his life. It wasn't much time, but he'd have to find a way.

LILY GROANED softly, then sat up and turned on the bedside lamp. She picked up her pillow and punched it, then finally tossed it on the floor. She'd been trying to go to sleep for the past hour, desperate to get at least some rest before she had to get up for her interview. But every time she closed her eyes, she saw his face.

She'd dreamed about the time she'd see him again, but her encounter with Aidan had been nothing like those dreams. She'd been so nervous, afraid to say anything that might bring up the past. But Lily wanted to put it all out there, to figure out how they'd gotten to this place after such a promising start.

She reached over, turned off the lamp and closed her eyes. But a frantic rapping at the door brought her upright. Lily scrambled out of bed and grabbed her robe, then hurried over to look out the peephole.

A gasp slipped from her lips and she stepped back. Aidan. It was nearly 2:00 a.m. What was he doing here? Lily undid the security latch and opened the door.

"Hi," he said, shifting back and forth on his feet.

Lily leaned out and looked up and down the empty hallway. "What are you doing here?"

"I just have to say something and then I'll go. I kind of got the idea that maybe you weren't too keen on dinner tomorrow night and then I started thinking you might cancel. Hey, I know things are a little strange between us."

"I know," Lily said, clutching at the front of her robe. "Why is that?"

"I've been trying to figure it out. I think it's because everything happened so fast. We didn't have a chance to learn the little stuff."

"Maybe that's it," Lily said. "I mean, we really started at the end and then tried to go back to the beginning. That doesn't work."

"And you can't learn the little stuff over the phone. We needed to be with each other for that." He paused. "But that's not what I came to say."

"It's all right," Lily said. "I don't need you to—"

"Just wait," he said. "Let me say this and then you can talk." He glanced over her shoulder. "Can I come in? This really isn't the kind of thing that should happen in the hallway."

Lily stepped back from the door and he walked inside. He turned around and faced her, his gaze searching her face. Raking his fingers through his hair, Aidan began to pace the room. "Just give me a second here while I gather my thoughts."

Lily sat down on the end of the bed and watched him. "It's such a coincidence you're here," she said.

"It is?"

Lily nodded, then picked up a small box from the bedside table. "I was shopping at an antique store yesterday and I found this. I thought I'd send it to you for Christmas, but now that you're here, I can give it to you in person." She handed him the box. "Go ahead, you can open it."

He pulled the lid off and picked through the tissue paper. Carefully, Aidan pulled out the cast-iron bank he'd described to her that day in Eastport, the bank he'd played with at his grandfather's house.

"I hope that's it," Lily said.

"This is it," he said.

"The funny thing is that it's made in America and I found it here. It was strange. It was up on a shelf in this shop in Piccadilly and I wasn't really even looking in that direction and then I just saw it. And I thought of you." She stood up and pointed to the figure. "The paint is original. That's important. It adds to the value."

"Thank you," Aidan said. "So I guess you still think of me occasionally."

"I think of you all the time," Lily admitted.

He carefully rewrapped the bank and set it on the dresser, then turned to her. "All right. Here it is. Lily, I love you. I think I fell in love with you the moment I kissed you on that plane. And I haven't stopped since."

She stared at him, wide-eyed, her hands clutched in her lap. Lily tried to maintain a calm facade, but her heart was beating so hard it felt as though it might burst out of her chest. "I—I don't know what to say."

"I know," Aidan said. "Big surprise. Maybe I should have worked into it a little slower, but I know what I want and I'm tired of wasting time."

Lily scrambled to explain her feelings. "I—I just wasn't expecting you to say that."

"Believe me, neither was I." He sat down beside her and cupped her face in his hands, pressing his forehead to hers. "I'm not sure what this means, Lily. Maybe it doesn't mean anything, but I know how I feel. And if we never see each other again after tonight, at least I said it. At least you know."

"I know," she said.

"Lily, I'm willing to work hard at it. I'll do whatever it takes. I can live in L.A. or New York, wherever you want. I'll get a job in television. I'll be home every night. We can find a house and start a life together."

Lily shook her head. "No."

"No to television? Or no to me?"

Lily jumped up from the bed and crossed the room to the closet. She pulled out her leather tote and searched in the front pocket until she found her little scrapbook. She walked back to the bed and sat down.

"I want to show you something," Lily explained. "I had to make this in my fear-of-flying class. We cut out pictures of things that made us feel happy, things we wanted in our lives. And when we're on a plane, we're supposed to take it out and focus on it." She paged through the little scrapbook. "Here. Here's a photo of you that I cut out of a magazine."

He stared down at it. "This was the premiere of my second film," he said.

"Yes. It's one of the only pictures of you where you're smiling. I liked that."

"And looking at my photo makes it easier for you to fly?"

Lily nodded. "But that's not what I wanted to tell you. I made this a year and a half ago."

"But you just added my picture?"

She shook her head. "No, it's been in there the whole time. You probably will think this is really strange and I don't blame you if you do, but since we're being honest, I want to tell you. I saw you in an airport lounge a year before we met on that plane. Miranda and I were going to Paris and she went over and introduced herself to you. She pointed me out and you looked over at me and smiled. And I fell in love." Lily giggled nervously. "I had the biggest crush on you. I know that's really weird for someone my age to say, but I did. I thought you were the perfect man."

"Did Miranda know this?"

"Yeah. She guessed by the way I was looking at you. So her manipulation went a little deeper than what you originally thought."

He paused, as if he were evaluating what she'd told him. "So, you've been in love with me for a year and a half?"

"Seventeen months to be exact," Lily said.

"And I've been in love with you since the moment I kissed you."

Lily smiled. "I guess so."

Aidan drew a deep breath and let it out slowly. "There's one other thing. I didn't just stumble on your book-signing," he said. "I knew you'd be there. I've been keeping track of your tour on your Web site. I know it sounds a little stalkerish, but it's not."

Reaching out, she took his hand and laced her fingers through his. "We made a pretty big mess of this, didn't we?"

"But we can fix it," Aidan said. "I want to, Lily. I want you in my life. I don't care what it takes, I'll make it happen."

Lily stood up in front of him and untied the belt of her robe. She shrugged out of it, letting it drop to the floor at her feet. Then she reached for the hem of her nightgown and pulled it over her head, tossing it aside.

Aidan reached out and splayed his hand across her stomach. "Are you trying to seduce me?" he asked.

Lily smoothed her hand over his cheek. "Yes, I am."

"Don't you think we should talk about this?"

She slowly shook her head. "We can talk later. I want to make love to the man I love."

He pulled her close and pressed his face into her stomach. "Promise me something, Lily."

Furrowing her fingers through his hair, she tipped his gaze up to meet hers. "Anything."

"I'm the first and last guy you use that book on, all right?"

Lily laughed. "I promise. I won't be seducing any more strangers on planes, or anywhere else for that matter."

Aidan stood and began to remove his clothes. When he was naked, he glanced at his watch before taking it off and setting it on the bed. "All right, my dear. You have ten minutes. And not a minute more."

He grabbed her waist and they tumbled onto the bed in a tangle of limbs. When his mouth found hers, Lily knew this was the only thing she needed in life. Aidan— his heart, his soul, his body, his love.

Her fantasy had become a reality and it was even better that she could have dreamed.

Epilogue

Next summer

AIDAN STOOD on the balcony and stared out at the Pacific. The water was a perfect shade of blue, reflecting the color of the cloudless sky. He drew a deep breath and tried to remember every detail. This was an important day. Maybe one of the most important of his life.

He turned and looked through the open doors into the living room of their Malibu house. Lily was curled up on the overstuffed sofa, the pages of her latest manuscript scattered around her.

Her first novel, *The Glitter Child,* was due to be published next month and he'd already secured an option on the film rights. The novel had created quite a buzz in Hollywood and the publicity machine was winding up.

He smiled to himself. Lily had come a long way since last summer. She wasn't different, just a little better at coping with the complexities of fame. She'd found a self-assurance that Aidan had come to admire. Yet, in their moments alone, she was sometimes still insecure and vulnerable.

They'd been living together since the previous Christmas, finding the Malibu beach house after they'd both returned from London. It was the perfect life, Aidan mused. When he was out of town on location, Lily would come with him. And when her publicity schedule was busy, he'd find a way to meet her wherever she was.

It had worked well so far. But Aidan still worried that something would come along to steal their happiness. He wanted to know that he and Lily would be together forever. Aidan reached in his pocket and pulled out the ring, the diamond flashing in the sunlight.

It was a risk. He knew how skittish she was when it came to the subject of marriage. But they loved each other and they belonged together. If Lily wasn't ready to accept that, then maybe he'd have to force the issue.

Aidan walked inside and Lily looked up. "What's wrong?" she asked, frowning.

"Nothing," he replied.

She shook her head. "You've been pacing around here all morning. Why don't you take a run on the beach? Get some exercise. Then we'll go have lunch."

"I don't need any exercise," he said. Aidan walked over to the mantel and picked up the mechanical bank she'd given him in London. They'd come so close to letting it all go.

He reached in his pocket and put the ring into the bank, then wandered over to the sofa. "Can you help me with this?"

Lily glanced up. "With what?"

"I want to get the money out of the bank, but I can't figure out how it works."

"Why do you want the money?"

"It's full. I can't put any more in."

"Just tip it over and shake it."

Aidan shook his head. She wasn't going to make this easy. "No, that won't work."

Lily sighed dramatically and grabbed the bank from his hands. She turned it upside down and pointed to the circular opening in the bottom. "You have to unscrew this," she said. "There's a little slot here. It looks like you can use a coin to twist it open."

"You do it," Aidan said.

Lily shook her head. "I'm trying to finish this chapter." She stared at him for a long moment. "Why are you acting so weird?"

Aidan reached into his pocket and found a penny, then handed it to her. Grudgingly, Lily unscrewed the bottom of the bank then held it out over the coffee table. The pennies scattered on the wood surface and a moment later, the ring fell out.

Lily blinked in surprise as she reached for it. "What's this?"

"Looks like a ring," Aidan said.

She examined it closely. "I can't believe someone left a ring in this bank. You'd think the shop owner would have found it. I know the price I paid didn't include this." Lily looked at him. "Do you think we should try to find out who owned the bank? Maybe try to get the ring back to them."

Aidan chuckled. So much for a cute romantic gesture. Why did these things always work so well in the movies and yet fail in real life? "I put the ring in the bank, Lily."

"But why would you—"

"Because I wanted you to find it. I wanted you to pick it up and realize that it was for you." He gently took it out of her hand and held it up. "It's yours. I bought it for you. I want you to marry me, Lily."

Her eyes were wide and her lips parted in disbelief. "You want to marry me?"

Aidan nodded. "Traditionally, you're supposed to give me an answer now. In the movies, the woman always starts crying and then she throws herself into the man's arms and says 'yes.' But by the way you're looking at me, I can see we're not going to follow the regular script."

"You want to marry me," she murmured, staring at the ring.

"I think we've established that," Aidan said.

She looked up at him and he saw tears glittering in her eyes. "Yes," she said. "Yes, I will marry you."

Lily tossed aside her manuscript, the pages flying to the floor, then launched herself across the sofa into his arms. Her lips met his and she gave him a long, delicious kiss.

When she finally drew back, Aidan captured her face in his hands and turned her gaze up to his. "Yes?"

She nodded. "Of course."

"You're not afraid that we'll end up like your parents?"

"I think we'll end up like your parents," she said.

"It's going to take work," Aidan warned. "We have to make sure we never forget that we come first, not our jobs."

"We can do that," Lily said. "I love you, Aidan. Nothing will ever change that."

He smoothed her hair away from her face, then kissed her gently. "And I love you, Lily." He took the ring off his index finger and slipped it onto her ring finger on her left hand. "I guess we're official," he said.

"We are."

"It was kind of romantic, wasn't it?" Aidan asked.

"I know how we can make it even more romantic," Lily whispered. "You can make love to me right now. You have ten minutes to convince me that you'll make a good husband." She stood up and grabbed his hand, pulling him to his feet.

Aidan chuckled, sweeping her into his arms as he stood. "Oh, darling, it's going to take a lot longer than ten minutes."

"A lifetime, then," Lily said, brushing her lips against his. "I'll give you a lifetime."

SPECIAL EDITION™

NEW YORK TIMES BESTSELLING AUTHOR

DIANA PALMER

A brand-new Long, Tall Texans novel

HEART OF STONE

Feeling unwanted and unloved, Keely returns
to Jacobsville and to Boone Sinclair, a rancher
troubled by his own past. Boone has always
seemed reserved, but now Keely discovers a
sensuality with him that quickly turns to love. Can
they each see past their own scars to let love in?

*Available September 2008
wherever you buy books.*

Silhouette®

Romantic

SUSPENSE

**Sparked by Danger,
Fueled by Passion.**

Cindy Dees
Killer Affair

Seduction in the sand…and a killer on the beach.

Can-do girl Madeline Crummby is off to a remote
Fijian island to review an exclusive resort, and she hires
Tom Laruso, a burned-out bodyguard, to fly her there
in spite of an approaching hurricane. When their plane
crashes, they are trapped on an island with a serial killer
who stalks overaffectionate couples. When their false
attempts to lure out the killer turn all too real, Tom and
Madeline must risk their lives and their hearts….

**Look for the third installment
of this thrilling miniseries,
available August 2008
wherever books are sold.**

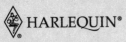
HARLEQUIN®

American ★ Romance®

CATHY MCDAVID
Cowboy Dad
THE STATE OF PARENTHOOD

Natalie Forrester's job at Bear Creek Ranch
is to make everyone welcome, which is an
easy task when it comes to Aaron Reyes—the
unwelcome cowboy and part-owner. His
tenderness toward Natalie's infant daughter
melts the single mother's heart. What's not
so easy to accept is that falling for him means
giving up her job, her family and the only
home she's ever known....

Available August
wherever books are sold.

LOVE, HOME & HAPPINESS

REQUEST YOUR FREE BOOKS!

2 FREE NOVELS
PLUS 2
FREE GIFTS!

HARLEQUIN®

Blaze™

Red-hot reads!

YES! Please send me 2 FREE Harlequin® Blaze™ novels and my 2 FREE gifts (gifts are worth about $10). After receiving them, if I don't wish to receive any more books, I can return the shipping statement marked "cancel." If I don't cancel, I will receive 6 brand-new novels every month and be billed just $4.24 per book in the U.S. or $4.71 per book in Canada, plus 25¢ shipping and handling per book and applicable taxes, if any*. That's a savings of 15% or more off the cover price! I understand that accepting the 2 free books and gifts places me under no obligation to buy anything. I can always return a shipment and cancel at any time. Even if I never buy another book, the two free books and gifts are mine to keep forever.

151 HDN ERVA 351 HDN ERUX

Name	(PLEASE PRINT)	
Address		Apt. #
City	State/Prov.	Zip/Postal Code

Signature (if under 18, a parent or guardian must sign)

Mail to the **Harlequin Reader Service:**
IN U.S.A.: P.O. Box 1867, Buffalo, NY 14240-1867
IN CANADA: P.O. Box 609, Fort Erie, Ontario L2A 5X3

Not valid to current subscribers of Harlequin Blaze books.

Want to try two free books from another line?
Call 1-800-873-8635 or visit www.morefreebooks.com.

* Terms and prices subject to change without notice. N.Y. residents add applicable sales tax. Canadian residents will be charged applicable provincial taxes and GST. Offer not valid in Quebec. This offer is limited to one order per household. All orders subject to approval. Credit or debit balances in a customer's account(s) may be offset by any other outstanding balance owed by or to the customer. Please allow 4 to 6 weeks for delivery. Offer available while quantities last.

Your Privacy: Harlequin Books is committed to protecting your privacy. Our Privacy Policy is available online at www.eHarlequin.com or upon request from the Reader Service. From time to time we make our lists of customers available to reputable third parties who may have a product or service of interest to you. If you would prefer we not share your name and address, please check here.

HARLEQUIN®

Blaze™

COMING NEXT MONTH

#411 SECRET SEDUCTION Lori Wilde
Perfect Anatomy, Bk. 2
Security specialist Tanner Doyle is an undercover bodyguard protecting surgeon Vanessa Rodriguez at the posh Confidential Rejuvenations clinic. Luckily, keeping the good doctor close to his side won't be a problem—the sizzling sexual chemistry between them is like a fever neither can escape....

#412 THE HELL-RAISER Rhonda Nelson
Men Out of Uniform, Bk. 5
After months of wrangling with her greedy stepmother over her inheritance, the last thing Sarah Jane Walker needs is P.I. Mick Chivers reporting on her every move. Although with sexy Mick around, she's tempted to give him something worth watching....

#413 LIE WITH ME Cara Summers
Lust in Translation
Philly Angelis has been in love with Roman Oliver forever, but he's always treated her like a kid. But not for long... Philly's embarking on a trip to Greece—to find her inner Aphrodite! And heaven help Roman when he catches up with her....

#414 PLEASURE TO THE MAX! Cami Dalton
Cassie Parker gave up believing in fairy tales years ago. So when her aunt sends her a gift—a lover's box, reputed to be able to make fantasies come true—Cassie's not impressed...until a sexy stranger shows up and seduces her on the spot. Now she's starring in an X-rated fairy tale of her very own.

#415 WHISPERS IN THE DARK Kira Sinclair
Radio talk show host Christopher Faulkner, aka Dr. Desire, has been helping people with their sexual hang-ups for years. But when he gets an over-the-air call from vulnerable Karyn Mitchell, he suspects he'll soon be the one in over his head....

#416 FLASHBACK Jill Shalvis
American Heroes: The Firefighters, Bk. 2
Firefighter Aidan Donnelly has always battled flames with trademark icy calm. That is, until a blazing old flame returns—in the shape of sizzling soap star Mackenzie Stafford! Aidan wants to pour water over the unquenchable heat between them. But that just creates more steam....

www.eHarlequin.com

HBCNM0708